P

A Gentle

An erotic epistolary novel that is more Victorian-like, more sentimental than a historical romance novel typically published today. It's different and entertaining. I enjoyed its difference and I also appreciated the author's unique perspective.~ *Whipped Cream*

Books by Natalie Dae

Anthologies

Bound to the Billionaire

Single Titles

A Gentleman's Harlot
That Filthy Book
Shades of Grey
Forced Assassin
Rude Awakening
Waiting for Him
Magenta Starling
Shadow and Darkness
Lincoln's Woman

A Gentleman's Harlot

ISBN # 978-1-78651-887-3

©Copyright Natalie Dae 2016

Cover Art by Posh Gosh ©Copyright 2016

Interior text design by Claire Siemaszkiewicz

Totally Bound Publishing

Published in 2016 by Totally Bound Publishing, Newland House, The Point, Weaver Road, Lincoln, LN6 3QN, United Kingdom.

Printed and bound in Great Britain by Clays Ltd, St Ives plc

A GENTLEMAN'S HARLOT

NATALIE DAE

Dedication

Sometimes I can't see the woods for the trees. It takes
a special pair of eyes to spot the things I just can't see
anymore after writing a book. Those special eyes belong to
my editor, Sue. She has an amazing ability, knows exactly
how I can fix things when I thought I couldn't, or I didn't
realise a little extra saucy and sexy was needed to give
the book more spark. Without her guidance, her way of
having me slapping my forehead and saying, "Now why
didn't I see that myself, hmmm?" A Gentleman's Harlot
would have been a lesser version than it is now.
So, Sue, my dear, I thank you.
For being the star that you are.

Prologue

The Diary of Seth Adams

October 1887

She rested beneath me on the bed, a high-class harlot, gazing into my eyes as though she loved me. Of course, I knew she did not, but she pretended because I paid her for the ruse. She was not the woman I wished her to be. I did not know her real name, only that she called herself Charlotte and that she accommodated me every time I called to make an appointment. An appointment, as though what I did with her was nothing more than a visit to the physician or to the tailor. Perhaps that made me feel better. Perhaps I knew what I did was wrong, taking a woman I did not love even though she had chosen her profession and was willing to offer her services.

She was not Pearl, the woman I coveted, although she did have the same red hair. Charlotte's splayed across the white, cotton-covered pillow in a pure, straight sheet, yet Pearl's, I imagined, would be a heap of riotous curls that would tangle with our lovemaking. I doubted I would ever get to see her that way, for if rumours were to be believed she hated me.

Charlotte tilted her head a little, the faux love in her light blue eyes turning to impatience along with a question. I guessed it to be: Why are you staring at me with your cock deeply seated inside, unmoving, looking as though you would rather be anywhere but here?

Was that true? Yes, I would rather not have that woman

beneath me, but a man had needs, and although I wished I did not visit the harlot, I had to slake the lust running through me somehow. My hand was not good enough, and I wanted no other "nice" woman except Pearl.

I feared I was destined to take my pleasure from women of the night for the rest of my life.

"What is the matter?" Charlotte asked, her voice tinged with a hard edge that made me wince. "You might be in my bed and in my cunt, but you are certainly *not* here."

"I am sorry. I—"

"Who is she?"

Her question did not startle me. She asked it often. Was it that obvious I was in love with someone else? I gave in and offered an explanation for the first time. "She is someone I wish to marry, but it will never happen."

"Pretend I am her. Please?"

I did so, bringing Pearl's face to mind, and grew harder. Charlotte lifted her slim legs and settled her heels at the base of my spine, trailed her hands up and down my back. I avoided looking directly at her face, half-closing my eyes to fool myself Pearl was there instead. It worked, and I concentrated on the redness of her hair, the curve where her neck met her shoulder. Kissing the soft hollow of her throat, I closed my eyes and pretended, dashing my tongue out to taste the delicate skin under my lips. Would Pearl taste like this? Did she wear scent that would tantalise me, make her instantly recognisable above all other women?

I shut away those musings, desire overtaking my idle mind. Charlotte moaned as I shunted in and out with sharp, brisk strokes, and I wondered if she faked the pleasure as well as the loving looks. It did not matter. I was here to put out the fire that had burned inside me ever since I had laid eyes on Pearl, and Charlotte was only a vessel. Wretched of me to think that way, but there you have it. Better that I kept my urges under control with a willing partner than approach Pearl and be rejected.

I could not bear that.

I pumped harder, lifting my torso away from Charlotte, and slid one hand up her belly to scoop a full breast. Caressing the swell, my thumb brushing over her soft nipple, I coaxed the nub into hardness. She closed her eyes, fingernails digging into my back and arched her neck. That slender throat enticed me, made me want to lick up the column and suckle her earlobe, and I gave in, relaxing into the act.

Charlotte's sheath contracted, gentle spasms that threatened to milk me of the seed that sat heavy in my bollocks. I visited only when I could hold back no longer, and it had been more than a month since I was last here. Her nipple grew more rigid, and I tweaked it between finger and thumb, twisting it a little the way she seemed to like. Another moan left her, and she stared at me, issuing a challenge to play a game — one we indulged in most times.

"Fuck me from behind," she said on an exhale. "At the window."

It was a risk, I knew that, knew it every time we did it, but a reckless part of me did not care. We might be seen, and that made our possibly irresponsible act all the more enticing. Here, with Charlotte, I was able to do things I doubted any wife would want to do, but I became excited, imagining Pearl was the kind of woman who would allow such guilty pleasures.

I drew out of Charlotte, my cock soaked in her juices, and stood at the foot of the bed, watching as she walked across the room. Hips swaying, she glanced at me over her shoulder, and for a moment, with the candlelight playing on her face, she looked like Pearl. I wanted her then, wanted this harlot so much my balls hurt, but I resisted following her. In this game, she dictated, she was the one who orchestrated how things went, and I was happy to defer to her.

She drew back the heavy red curtains, her hair swishing the same way as the fabric — left to right, left to right — then pressed her hands to the wide, cream-painted sill. She jutted her arse out, widening her legs as far as they would go, and dropped her head so her hair hung either side of her face.

Her rounded buttocks called to me, begged to be stroked, but I remained where I was to take in the sight of her. Standing like that, she could have been any woman, could even have been my Pearl. The thought of that had my hardness bobbing, straining. A curious sensation crept from my root to the tip, an almost burning rush of bliss that could have made me come had I allowed it. But I did not. I wanted to be inside her. Wanted skin on skin and to hear the gentle slap as our bodies met with each of my thrusts.

Charlotte sighed, with longing or impatience I did not know, yet still she did not call for me to join her. I stared at the valley of her arse and down to the darkness between her legs, knowing the wet folds there were ready to receive my throbbing cock. That her slit was so moist, that if I touched her my fingers would come away dripping. I almost groaned but held it back. I did not want her to know how much she teased me, how much I wanted to sink inside her damp heat to thrust in and out until we cried out with the headiness of it all.

The flame from a candle on the bedside to our left flickered, giving a brief glimpse of how drenched she was. Her juices sparkled on her inner thighs, and I re-evaluated my earlier thought that she faked her enjoyment with me. No woman was so wet when she did not want a man. The idea that she enjoyed my attentions brought a strong surge of longing to my cock, and I resisted palming myself. The temptation to fist out my desire was immense, yet holding back gave a greater yearning to plunge inside her and ride her as though it was the last fuck I would ever have.

I could not deny that despite how I felt about Pearl, Charlotte had the ability to coax feelings in me that no other woman had in the bedroom. I had sampled many but now always chose Charlotte. She was the sole woman in my sexual life.

"Come here." The words were ragged, torn.

I strode across the room though I wanted to run. I stood

behind her, my feet planted firmly on the polished wooden boards. Her arched back showcased the dips and swells of her spine, and I reached out to run my fingertip down the column to the apex of her arse cleft. She shivered then gasped, pushing her bottom out farther. Her slit glistened again, only for a second. Then the cavity became a mystery, something I had to imagine as darkness seeped between her legs once more.

Without waiting for her instruction, I took the candle from beside the bed and placed it on the sill to give me some light. I kneeled behind her, running my hands up her inner thighs. I parted her folds to take in their beauty and eyed her opening that waited for my cock to fill it. Her bud was swollen, its perfect roundness shining in the candlelight. My mouth watered, and I leant forward to flick my tongue out and taste the salty liquid that coated her.

It is not true all women taste the same. Charlotte's juices are strong, the scent of her almost overpowering, enough to send a man insane. I breathed her in, my nose touching the lower curve of her hole, and tongued her needy bud. She gasped, sucked in a breath, and I let her cream infuse my tongue. She pushed back, apparently wanting more pressure, and I gave it. The sensation of being the one who controlled her release coursed through me, targeting my cock and bollocks the most.

I could take no more. Standing, I smoothed my hands down her back, then up again to her shoulders. I moved forward so my tip butted her entrance, the heat there a cap of warm pleasure. Her breaths came heavy and hard, and I glanced around her to see she scrabbled at the sill, her fingertips finding no purchase. Yes, she enjoyed me, enjoyed my visits, and that knowledge gave me the impetus to shove inside her right up to the hilt.

She cried out, lifted her head then dropped it again, her long, drawn-out groan stoking the burning fire that raged through me. I held tight to her shoulders to give me leverage and began a frantic rhythm. My arse cheeks clenched with every jerk, the clamp of her channel squeezing me so hard I followed the urge to move faster.

Sweat broke out on my brow and back, and I listened to that sound I loved so much—slap, slap, slap—where my skin met with hers. I looked down to see my length sliding in and out of her. The sight was so erotic, my cock soaking, my bollocks swaying, that the inevitable happened far quicker than I would have liked. I gritted my teeth as the familiar feeling swamped me, the tingling that started in my balls and travelled up my shaft. I closed my eyes briefly to better revel in the sensations, and brought Pearl to mind.

Pearl was the woman I plundered. Pearl was the woman who stood at the window, her legs spread, her wet hole clamping around me. Pearl was the woman who gave herself to me freely, who moaned and gasped as I picked up speed.

"Oh!" Charlotte said, that one word the length of many. "Oh, Seth. You feel so good."

She knew what to say and when.

I slid my hands to her waist, gripping where it spread out to full, wide hips. Each time I pushed inside her, I brought her backward on to my cock, the strength of my actions not enough, not as much as I wanted. But what *did* I want?

That was easy. I wanted to shove so hard she could not hold back any longer. I wanted to hear our skin slapping louder, the time between contact minimal. I wanted it fast, aggressive, both of us sweating, Charlotte's breasts bouncing, her breathing hitched.

And then it came, the point of no return. A massive rush of desire overtook me a moment before my burning seed jetted out of me and into her. She took one hand from the sill, and it disappeared between her legs. I watched her elbow jerk as she fondled herself, panting, groaning when her release came. I emptied several streams into her, the passage slick, the wetness a further excitement that urged one last, short spurt to join the rest.

As Charlotte's groans tapered away, I slowed to a stop.

Breathing heavily, I stared over her and out the window at the street. Houses stood opposite, their shapes darker than the night surrounding them, candlelight doused as the occupants slept. I always visited deep into the night to reduce the possibility of being seen. Although it was not unheard of for someone of my standing to take prostitutes, I would rather my guilty secret remained within these walls. So why, then, did I play this perverse game at the window?

I withdrew, turning away and walking to the sideboard on the other side of the room. I washed my cock, still tender from the assault I had given it, and soaped my balls. Cold reality came then, as it always did, and I felt ashamed that I was here. That I had taken a woman who was not Pearl.

It is strange, the way I think of her as though she were mine. As though my being here means I have sinned, taking another woman behind Pearl's back. But of course, that was not so. The woman I long for has no clue I ache to have her — not just in my bed but in my life as a permanent fixture. And she would not want me should I present myself at her home and ask to court her. Once she found out my name, I would be banished, told never to return.

The swish of fabric drew me from my thoughts, and I turned to see Charlotte behind me holding a nightgown to her breasts. I smiled, a little sadly to be honest, and took the dirty water past her and over to the window. I drew up the lower half and threw the water outside, leaving the window open. I returned the bowl to the sideboard where she still waited, then moved away from her — the penetrating stare she gave me put me ill at ease. I guessed she was in the mood to talk.

"You know, we could make a good life together, Seth, if only you would put her out of your mind."

I sighed quietly and went to the chair beside the door. I dressed with my back to her while she poured fresh water into the bowl and began washing. I wished the conversation that was sure to follow would not. "It is not as simple as that. She consumes me."

Perhaps I had hurt her with that comment, for she took some time before she spoke again.

"But you do not know anything about her, only what you have heard."

"I know enough. And when I first saw her...*that* was enough for me to know that I..."

What was the point in trying to explain? It sounded insane, that just the sight of a woman had told me I was meant to be with her. That seeing her wavy red hair, so stark against the black of mourning as she stood beside her father's open grave, let me know that I needed to feel those tresses running through my fingers. Love at first sight. It happened. It existed.

"You consume *me*," Charlotte said.

I was so shocked I spun to face her. My mouth dropped open, and words failed to come. I did not know what to say.

"I entertain only you, Seth. Did you not know that? Ever since your first visit, I have refused any other man." She laughed quietly when I did not answer, her dusky pink lips forming a tight smile. "That I am the madam gives me the right to choose." I still did not answer, and she rushed on. "I thought I could make you love me. Silly of me, I know." She blushed and turned away, scooping up her silk nightgown and putting it on.

No, it was not silly. Was I not doing the same thing? Hoping that one day Pearl would love me? I understood Charlotte more than she could imagine, and realised that my visiting here again would be a mistake. And a cruelty to Charlotte.

I finally found my voice. "Charlotte, I am terribly sorry. I had no idea you felt this way. I shall not come here again. It is not right that I do so now. You must forget me, forget you ever met me."

She made to move forward, hands raised as if she were about to cradle my face and kiss me, something she had tried to do before but I had rebuffed. Kissing was too intimate. The only woman I wanted to kiss did not want to

14

kiss me.

"No, please," I said, holding up one hand. "I cannot visit here knowing what I do now. I would be giving you false hope. I must leave." I fumbled into my black coat then took out some notes, holding them out to her with a surprisingly shaky hand.

She stared at the money, a livid red blush staining her cheeks. "I do not want it. I have never wanted it. Only you." She presented her back to me, the conversation over.

I felt wretched as I left her room, her whorehouse, and blundered out onto the street. I had used her for what she offered, visited her as a business transaction and nothing more, yet all that time she…

Jesus Christ, what have I done?

Feelings of having duped Pearl took a firm grip of me as I staggered down the lonely street like a man who had sunk one too many ales. It was a stupid notion, I knew, but she was so firmly ensconced in my mind as my woman that the feeling was hard to shake. I had justified my visits to Charlotte as only taking care of my needs, but now I saw how wrong I had been.

I vowed to meet Pearl one day, to show her that I was not the man she thought I was. That I could love her, give her a good life, and have her love me back.

Until then, my fist would be my only companion in the bedroom.

Chapter One

November 8th, 1888

Pearl Lewis looked up from her sewing, needle poised above the small square of white fabric. "What did you just say?" She stared at Frances, one of two childhood friends who had come for afternoon tea, taking in her flushed cheeks and devilish smile. Frances's words had held such a hint of daring, of non-conformation, that Pearl wanted her to repeat them just so she could revel in them again.

Sitting on Pearl's left, Frances smiled and shook her riot of blonde curls back from her face, the corn colour enhanced by the sunlight streaming through the two windows behind their wing chairs. "I *said*, would you not just love to visit the new men's club and become one of their women?"

Pearl tried to hide a smile. Frances's shocking statements never failed to amuse her. She dropped her needle to her lap and covered her mouth with one hand. Her cheeks flushed at the thoughts Frances's suggestion brought, and she closed her eyes for a moment to sift through the images. Men fondling women—*Oh God, how...naughty!*—women touching men *there*, and several people at once, all naked, all having...sex.

Pearl opened her eyes to find her other friend's face directly in front of hers, Elizabeth's black hair hanging rod straight as she hunkered down and placed her hands on her knees. Her dark blue eyes were hooded due to the unsightly frown she wore, and Pearl started, slapping her hand over her heart.

"Oh, you scared me, Beth! I did not expect to see you

there like that."

Elizabeth leaned closer, head tilted, the ornately carved mahogany mantelpiece behind her framing her as though she were a painting. Elizabeth regarded her with such scrutiny Pearl grew uncomfortable.

"What did you see just then?" Elizabeth asked, her voice quiet, a hint of reproach in her tone. The case clock beside the crackling fire ticked for several seconds, and her mouth formed a tight pink line that did not become her. She whispered, "With your eyes closed. What did you see?"

Pearl cleared her throat and looked away from Elizabeth to Frances, who smothered a giggle behind her long, slender fingers. Pearl tried to convey that she needed help by widening her eyes, but Frances made much ado about continuing with her sewing, pursing her lips in concentration.

"I...I really do not think," Pearl turned back to Elizabeth, "it is proper for me to say."

Elizabeth widened her eyes and reared back, as though in shock that Pearl had refused to share her thoughts.

Pearl rushed on. "Oh, it is not because I do not want to share. I do, but you are so...sensitive about certain things that I would hate for you to leave here somewhat... disturbed."

"Disturbed?" Elizabeth stood abruptly and paced up and down the cream and blue patterned rug before the fireplace, her dark green dress swishing with each step. "Whatever do you mean?" She paused, staring first at Frances, then at Pearl. "Oh! You were not thinking...you did not...?"

Pearl clamped her lips closed, nodded and looked down at her lap, picking up her sewing. "I thought things I perhaps should not have, Beth." She jabbed the needle through the material—a handkerchief she was embroidering on each corner—and pricked her finger. "Ouch!" She jumped up, placed her sewing on the chair seat and popped her finger into her mouth. The taste of copper flooded her tongue.

"Really, Pearl! You are almost as bad as Frances." Elizabeth paced again, throwing an appalled glance at the blonde. "I wish you two would hurry along and get married like me. Then perhaps you would not wish to discuss such a thing as being a gentleman's harlot. Pearl, your mother and father would spin in their graves if they heard even a snippet of the conversations you two have, and it is a blessing your aunt is old and easily fooled. If she were to walk past this door she would never let you leave this house!"

Pearl chanced a peek at Frances, who eyed her from beneath lowered lashes, her lack of control obvious as her cheeks reddened and her mouth curved. Frances released a peal of laughter, throwing her head back.

Pearl giggled, unable to remain chastised. "Oh, Beth, please! Surely you know Frances was only talking. It is not as though she intends to *do* such a thing." Pearl looked at Elizabeth.

She stalked back to her seat and sat with dignity and grace. "One never knows with Frances," she muttered, lifting her reticule on to her lap and dropping her sewing inside. "And, much as I love you both, I really do not feel I can visit for afternoon tea once a week if the conversation is going to revolve around things like…that. The gentleman's club of which you speak is situated in a terrible part of the city, so I heard. Frances, how you could even contemplate visiting such an establishment, even if it were in a respectable part of London, is beyond me." She glared at Frances, then stood and hung her bag over her forearm. "And to think only an hour ago we were discussing the terrible murders that have been occurring," she paused for her usual dramatic effect, "in the *very same area!*" Sharp lines marred her forehead. "I shall wait out in the foyer. Gerald will be here shortly to collect me." She flounced from the room, shutting the door loudly behind her.

Pearl stared at the door, her mouth hanging slightly open. Frances's laughter filled the room again, and Pearl turned to look at her, ready to admonish the young woman, but she failed. Her own laughter spilled, loud and hearty, and tears welled in her eyes.

"Oh, we should not laugh at her, Frances."

Frances composed herself and adjusted the neckline of her rose-pink dress, patting it once satisfied it lay in place. "She has become so priggish since she married Gerald that I cannot stand it. I say these things to rile her, you know."

"I am well aware of that." Pearl smiled. She took her sewing from her seat and put it on the round occasional table between their chairs. She glanced out the window at the front lawn, spying Gerald's coach trundling up the curved driveway. "He is here. Should I see her out?"

Frances snorted. "Oh, leave Mrs Prissy to see herself out. If she sets eyes on us any more today she is likely to explode. Besides, your aunt might have waylaid her. I hear someone talking."

Pearl smoothed her hands along her thighs, the skirt of her dark red dress rustling beneath her touch. She caught sight of a wisp of her wavy russet hair hanging loose from the bun she'd laboriously put it in this morning, and tucked it behind her ear. Who would want a redhead for a wife? Certainly no one she had encountered lately. Aunt Edith had asked men to call on Pearl's behalf, trying to marry her off and make her appear decent, but no man had appealed. Also, each man had commented on her hair, declaring that she must be foul-tempered, a woman he would not care to try and tame.

Pearl sighed, went to the window, and watched Elizabeth, now swaddled in a long thick coat, walk down the stone steps and on to the drive. She took Gerald's hand, and he kissed hers before helping her up into the carriage.

Do I want that? The touch of a man's lips on my skin?

Yes, she did. With another sigh, she turned from the window to stare at the bookcases either side of the door. She had read every book, some twice. Her life since her parents had died had become so tedious, each day the same, melting into the next without anything of import happening.

Unless I count these afternoon teas.

"Frances, I am bored with my life. Since Mother and Father…" She turned to face her friend. "What about you?"

Frances smiled brightly over her shoulder. "Well, you know me. Always smiling. Always happy. Good old Frances." She sighed and a touch of sadness flitted across her face. "Actually, I *am* bored, but I do *not* want to get married. Not yet. I want…something else first. Something so frowned upon, so deliciously naughty that if anyone were to find out I would be banished from their circles." She stood and twirled across the rug. "Oh, I want to *live*, Pearl. To have a secret, something to look forward to." Clutching her hands to her chest, she stared at Pearl, eyes over-bright and cheeks flushed. "Do you understand?"

Pearl sat in her chair, propped her elbow on the wooden chair arm and cradled her chin. Frances's inference struck her, and Pearl rose abruptly, rushing towards her friend. "Did you mean what you said earlier? Is *that* what you are saying?"

Frances nodded, her blonde curls bouncing. "Yes! Oh, the drama of being in the thick of it, the terror of being in a place of ill repute, murders being committed right outside the very door. Would it not be such *fun?*"

They stared at one another, Frances clearly waiting for an answer, Pearl unsure which one to give. Should she admit the idea of visiting the men's club intrigued her? Should she tell her friend that she lay awake at night, tormented by visions of men making love to her, touching her in places only she had touched? She trusted Frances without question, so to admit such things would not be so bad, but to actually go to the club in a place of squalor and debauchery?

"How would we do that?" Pearl asked, heat flooding her cheeks. "How would we get inside?"

"Oh, I have already looked into that. I applied for us to be waitresses." Frances jigged up and down, clapping and smiling. "We start tonight!"

"What? Oh my goodness!" Pearl gripped Frances's upper

arms. Her stomach tightened, and her heart raced. "Tell me you did not. Tell me you are playing one of your silly jokes."

Frances laughed. "For our secret life, your name is Lily and mine is Violet. Is that not a scream?"

"Oh, Lord. You are serious." Staggering backward, Pearl plopped into her chair and gaped at Frances, her breaths coming hard and fast. She clutched the chair arms, fingers curling over the edges. "What on earth possessed you? How did you know I would agree?"

Frances floated towards her, kneeling on the polished floorboards to take Pearl's hands in hers. "Because, dear friend, underneath it all we are both *very* naughty girls! Besides," she stood again and danced in a circle, arms out by her sides, "it is not as though we will be doing anything remotely like the *other* women there. Is it?"

"Other women?"

"Yes. Those free with their favours. Unless—"

"Frances, stop! You are not seriously considering doing *that*, are you?"

"Why not? Would you not like to sample a man and know what it is all about before you marry?" Frances walked along the rug, fingertip skating across the mantelshelf. "I realise being chaste is something to be expected, but it is all so…so *boring!* And horse riding is a valid excuse for things not being quite right down below on your wedding night."

Pearl swallowed down the urge to laugh, even though fear at where they were possibly headed threatened to overtake her. Frances felt the same way she did. They had been brought up knowing it was not correct to do this, was not correct to do that, but something inside Pearl screamed for her to take control of her own destiny, to do what she wanted to do, consequences be damned.

"Lily it is, then," she said, standing and walking to the window. She sat on the sill, staring at the grounds. The shrubbery that separated their driveway from the lawn was barren of leaves or flowers, all pointy branches that spoke of autumn leaving and winter coming. The vast expanse of grass that stretched to the tall bushes that bordered their property was brushed with a kiss of frost. Even the main length of gravel drive to her right, which snaked in a slightly wavy line until it reached the road, glistened with white sprinkles. The cold season had fully arrived, and long days stuck inside lay ahead until spring came once more. "How many nights will we work?" She faced Frances, who strode to the other window and perched on the sill, pressing her nose to the glass. Her breath steamed the pane, and Pearl laughed at how her friend just did not give a damn.

I want to be like her. Like the me I am inside.

"As many as you like, Lily love," she said in a broad, affected London accent. "If you only want the one, then one is all you'll have. But if you fancy a bit of tuppin' seven nights a week, we'll make a woman of the night out of you yet!"

Pearl gasped then blushed. Frances's take on the lower classes was so real she almost believed she had not been raised by upper class people. Could Pearl speak like that? Act differently? And what if she encountered someone she should not? "What if we get recognised, Frances?"

Standing, Frances planted her hands on her hips. "It's Violet to you, my darlin', and we'll be careful, don't you worry about that. We'll have so much paint on our faces men'll be hard pressed to know us."

"And what will we wear? What time will we go? How will you get out without anyone seeing? And how will we get there and back safely?" Panicked, Pearl laced her fingers together and squeezed.

"That, my dear, is what we're about to discuss. So, give yer maid a call for some more of that good old Rosie Lee, and we'll get down ter business!"

* * * *

Pearl shivered and wrapped her black coat tighter around

her. She stood at the end of her driveway, hidden from the house by the trunk of a huge oak and a long evergreen hedge. She stared into the darkness, waiting for the glow of a carriage light to break through the gloom.

We have to be insane doing this. What was I thinking, to agree to such a thing?

She huffed out a breath, bubbling excitement churning her stomach despite her self-chastisement. It would not hurt for one night, would it? Playing another role, being someone else for a few hours? Frances had assured her there was plenty of face paint at the men's club in the large dressing room the women used. How did she know? The thought of all the women sharing one space appalled and enthralled Pearl at the same time. She could not imagine! Their dresses awaited them, and they would change from their clothing into something more revealing. Could Pearl do that? Show off her cleavage as Frances had said they must? Oh, she wanted to, more than anything she wanted to shirk society's rules and just be who she was inside, but the years of conforming ensured that her mind protested, even though her heart argued back.

One night is all I ask. One night tasting the fruits of another world.

Faint hoof beats filtered through the night, and Pearl peered down the road. The foggy carriage light grew larger as the vehicle approached, and she drew in a deep breath to steady her nerves. Frances was taking the biggest risk. She had planned to steal out of her home after pretending to retire early, escaping via the rear door the servants used. If her parents went to her room… *Oh, God. What if they find her gone? And Frances paying the groom to take his carriage out on an imaginary errand… If he gets caught out on his ruse…*

She peeked around the tree trunk and glanced at the house, her worries somewhat eased when she saw her home stood in darkness. It appeared as a silhouette, nothing like the sand-coloured building it was by daylight. The faint moon barely highlighted several chimneys poking into the sky, and the front door with its stone overhang supported by two columns had seemingly vanished.

Aunt Edith would not have heard Pearl leave, being hard of hearing or so she said, and their maid, Annabel, lived elsewhere, coming to the house early in the morning to make breakfast. She was safe for now.

The carriage wheels crunching on the uneven road drew her attention, and Pearl turned back, steeling herself for what was to come. Her heart! She would swear it beat too fast. To go into the centre of London when the female residents lived in fear was absurd.

But we are going anyway. What is wrong with us?

The carriage drew to a halt, the two black horses snorting, sending grey clouds from their nostrils up into the air. The animals hoofed the ground, heads bobbing, bridles tinkling, and the driver looked down at her, winking and tipping his hat.

"Miss Frances is inside, Miss Pearl. In you get."

Swallowing, Pearl gave a wobbly smile and opened the carriage door. Frances sat in the darkness, and Pearl could only imagine the impish grin she was sure beamed on her friend's face. She climbed inside, sitting on the opposite seat, and pulled the door closed. Frances's laughter jingled, and Pearl loosed some of her own, frightened out of her wits yet looking forward to their adventure.

"We are surely mad, Frances." Pearl hugged herself, the carriage pulling away and jolting her forward before rocking her back against the seat.

"Violet, Lily. From now on, we use our new names." She giggled again. "Is this not *so* amusing? I feel alive for the first time." She paused, then, "My parents think I have a headache."

"God, Fran—Violet. Think of the scandal if they discover you are gone and find out where we are. What will we do?" Pearl laced her fingers, wishing she had thought to wear gloves, and twiddled her thumbs.

"Is that not what makes this outing so exciting? Is that not what we wanted? A change from the usual drudgery we endure every day?"

"Yes, but—"

"Oh, hush and enjoy yourself."

Pearl rolled up the blind at the window and stared through the glass. The dirty brown sky grew dirtier the farther they travelled, the streets of inner city London fast approaching. She had not visited London by night for quite some time—it just was not the done thing unless she was being escorted to the theatre or a restaurant, which was a rare occurrence—and the thought of being out unchaperoned in such a dangerous part of the city twisted her stomach. The men's club was situated in Whitechapel, and she wondered why gentlemen wanted to visit a place like that. Was the draw of women eager to satisfy their needs stronger than their distaste at mixing with such females?

I am a terrible person for thinking this way. Those women cannot help where they live, which class they belong to, any more than I can help being born into mine.

Ashamed of herself—for had she not contemplated, if only for a moment, experiencing something those women experienced every night?—Pearl inhaled a steady breath then said, "Will we be safe? With that man roaming the streets… What if your groom is not waiting for us when we are ready to return home?"

"Stop fretting, Lily. Luke will wait in the yard behind the club. And yes, before you ask, he is aware of what we are doing. As you know, I have known him all my life and he keeps many of my secrets. He will not leave until we are ready. Besides, he will not get paid if he does."

Pearl nodded. Frances calling her Lily had sounded strange, and she rolled the name around in her mind, hoping she did not forget and give her real name if a man should ask. And *would* a man ask? Would he think her a loose woman, confusing her role as waitress with something more? Her stomach rolled over again, and she focused on the passing scenery, eyes widening as the carriage entered

Whitechapel. Anxious, she was tempted to unroll the window blind and block the unpleasantness outside, but the lure of studying Commercial Street proved too much to ignore.

She shuddered, thinking of how close they were to Mitre Square, the scene where Catherine Eddowes had been found in the early hours of September 30th. Pearl had read the newspapers, aghast that a man could slay women in the manner he had, eviscerating them, mutilating them and, if rumour was to be believed, taking internal body parts to sell on the American market. What fellow did such a thing?

No woman of the night was safe at present, yet still females loitered on Commercial Street, standing in the shadows only to step out on the path as the carriage approached. They appeared to wear every item of clothing they owned, to keep out the chill no doubt, and Pearl felt guilty that she wore such a fine coat and a beautiful dress. That she was about to play at being like those women, who offered themselves in order to earn money for food, or, as Elizabeth had pointed out earlier, money for drink.

"They are not like us, Pearl," she had said, curling her top lip in distaste. "They are disgusting. Gerald says they deserve to be killed, that they are asking for death. What kind of woman takes to the streets in the first place, let alone when a murderer is out there, ready to kill them in the darkness after he tricks them into thinking they have a genuine customer? Do they not have any morals? Do they not care that they have left their children at home alone, in filthy little hovels fit for no human being?"

Pearl had stared at Elizabeth then, horrified at her friend's opinion. Surely some of those women cared for their children and worked the way they did only out of necessity?

Thoughts of Catherine Eddowes and the news reports tugged at Pearl's mind. The woman's murder had stood out above the others, filling Pearl with pity, for the prostitute had been found wearing a skirt patterned with Michaelmas daisies and golden lilies. At the time, Pearl had wondered if the skirt had belonged to the woman from brand-new or whether she had accepted it as a hand-me-down or had bought it in Spitalfields Market. Had she felt pretty when wearing it? Did it make up for the fact that she wore men's lace-up boots and a man's vest? And the white-handled knife she had carried—clearly she had not been able to use it in time.

Dear God, the poor woman. I feel so guilty about what we are doing. So very guilty.

Pearl opened her mouth to tell Frances she could not go on, to yell for Luke to turn the carriage around and take her back home, but no words came out. Instead, she stared at Christ Church steeple towering regally in the darkness and silently prayed that the prostitutes were resting in peace and the dreadful man who had killed them would be caught soon.

The carriage turned down one of the streets that stemmed from Commercial, and Pearl exhaled through pursed lips, erasing the terrible thoughts from her mind and concentrating on the night ahead. Only one evening, that was all she would work, then she would go back home to cherish their hours of devilry for the rest of her life. She rolled down the window blind and stared ahead, just making out Frances's face, the spill of hair falling over her chest, the hood of her cloak covering the top of her blonde head.

"We are nearly there," Frances said with a sigh. "I will admit to being nervous now. How are you feeling, Lily?"

"Nervous. Frightened. Ashamed."

"Ashamed? Oh, do not think like that. At least not until afterwards." She chuckled. "Think of the men. The attention. Our audacity!"

Pearl caught on to Frances's excitement and nodded, praying her heart would slow down. "One night, Frances, and that is all."

"Violet, Lily. My name is Violet."

27

Chapter Two

The Diary of Seth Adams

November 8th, 1888

Who would have thought that I would open a men's club in such a grubby part of the city? Who would have thought I would have opened one at all after the debacle of visiting Charlotte? I certainly would never have entertained it had I not taken to the streets of Whitechapel a month past with Kenneth, the man I employ to run my brewery, the man who has become a firm friend.

We had decided on our destination that evening out of curiosity, wanting to visit the grim place where women had been slain, our consciences piqued by the macabre, the wretchedness reported in the newspapers. Something about visiting the public houses frequented by the lower classes intrigued me, a pastime I had never indulged in before. Kenneth, however, had, and he assured me in his Irish brogue that my eyes as well as my mouth would be opened wide.

And he had been correct. Each place we visited proved worse than the last. Women drank like men, tossing back tankards of ale as though born to it, their manner so unrefined I blinked several times in my growing stupor that such vixens existed. They were, for the most part, filthy and unkempt, and exhibited none of the staid decorum I was used to. This alone both amused and fascinated me, and I will admit to being a little ashamed that such people drew me. How could I *not* feel this way? I own a large brewery, am a man of some standing in society due to who my parents are—Mother is a lady, Father a government gentleman—and I was reared by a nanny who followed society's rules to the letter.

How then, could a man such as I even contemplate a visit to Whitechapel? Why would I even want to go? I put it down to pure inquisitiveness, the need to see how the other half live, albeit the half who get through their days semi-starved and their nights decidedly drunk. But more than that, I wished to do something with my wealth to help these people, and there, as we wove in loose-limbed zigzags along Commercial Street to the Princess Alice public house, my new venture was born.

A woman of the night had boldly stepped into our path, halting our progress and jamming one hand on her slender hip. Her face bore traces of filth—she had not washed in a week, I would wager—and eyed us with the look of one who knew, if we took her up on her offer of a few moments down an alley, she would make a pretty penny.

"All right, misters?" she had asked, nodding to each of us in turn, the whites of her eyes standing out against the dirt of her face.

Kenneth had glanced sideways at me. His expression startled me, for he looked stricken, horrified that a woman as pretty as she had been reduced to this. He shook his head as though to clear it of thoughts he had no business entertaining.

"Evening," he had said, smiling.

"Want a tuppin'?" she had asked, not a trace of embarrassment on her face, her mass of jet black curls spiralling over breasts covered in some form of ticking jacket. It appeared she had made it herself, what with the rough, uneven stitching. "It'll be quick." She sniffed. "Won't interrupt your night much, and I'm cheap at half the price." She smiled, showing a mouth where a full set of teeth had once resided, some now unfortunately missing or chipped, their colour bordering on brown.

29

My heart had gone out to her. I thought of the prostitutes Charlotte employed, so different to this woman here. Charlotte's "girls" had decent board and lodging, did not have to trudge up and down the streets looking for business. The business came to them, and Charlotte ensured they never suffered any harm.

I stepped forward, hand outstretched. I had the absurd idea that I could help her, stop the madness her existence had become, and give her a better life. Whether she would take it remained to be seen. The lower classes were fiercely proud and did not take kindly to handouts. They would steal, oh yes, they would steal all right, but taking something for nothing from the likes of me?

She had curled her fingers around my palm and curtsied, cocking her head to one side. "My, you're a fine one, you are. Reckon you'd be a ripper if I were to get you into a bed!" She blinked, realising what she had said, and stepped back, bright blue eyes clouding to the colour of pewter. "You ain't him, are you? That ripper?"

"No," I said, giving her hand a little squeeze before releasing it. "Neither one of us is him. Here." I dug my hand into my trouser pocket and brought out my wallet. "If only for tonight, take yourself away from here. Go home or wherever it is safe and rest easy." I pulled out a five-pound note and held it out to her. "Please. Take it."

She had stared at it, her eyes wide and her mouth a perfect O of surprise. I felt...God, I felt like I had done something good, gone some way into changing this night for a woman who undoubtedly trawled these terrible streets just to earn a living. But upon seeing her face, screwed up now and giving me reason to believe she verged on scratching my eyes out, doubt intruded.

"You're pulling my leg, ain't you?" she asked, regarding the note I still held as though it would disappear if she pulled her gaze away. "There ain't no man I ever met on this earth who would give me a fiver for nothin'. Come on, down the alley there, and I'll earn that money good and proper."

I flapped the note then pressed it into her hand. "No. Just take it. Go on home."

She scrunched the money into her fist, and tears filled her eyes. Her face smoothed out, and she gulped in a breath. "Mister, I—"

"Go home," I ordered, harsher than I had intended. Her plight had burrowed into me, affected me more than I could ever have imagined, and I clenched my jaw, waving for her to move along. I gripped Kenneth's arm and steered him towards the Princess Alice, willing myself not to look back and praying she would remain safe until the killer who stalked these streets had been apprehended. No words were necessary to explain why I had acted as I had done, for Kenneth nodded every so often and smiled, and I knew he would have done the same.

Once inside among men and women of similar standing to the prostitute outside, we supped from our ale tankards in silence, absorbing our surroundings and what we had witnessed so far. How had I been so blind as to think the tales of this area were just that, stories of slovenly women and ribald men, untruths told to us via newspapers? And did I not provide some of the ale that aided these people in their quest for nightly oblivion? Was I not to blame, in some part, for helping them become as drunk as I was?

Angered at myself, I gulped the remaining ale down my throat and staggered out into the night, leaning on the wall of the Princess Alice, staring at the sights before me. Women prowled, skulking in the darkness of shadowed doorways, plying their trade to whichever male happened by. Was one of those men *him*? The man who had spawned terror into the hearts of everyone in London?

I did not doubt he was out that night—do not doubt he is out there this night too—and I shuddered at the thought. Kenneth joined me outside, propping himself up against the wall beside me, nodding to himself as if he had an internal conversation playing in his mind.

"We could help them," he said presently, staring at a young woman disappearing down an alley with a man old enough to be her father. "Open a whorehouse where they can work in safety." His accent thickened. "Oh aye, I know it isn't proper, but it's something to think about. A gentleman's club, we can call it, and the women could be employed, cleaned up."

I sighed. "But these women... *Can* they be cleaned up? Do they even *want* to work in such a place? The streets are a great lure. They can escape quickly should the bobbies turn up. A place like you suggest... And what of me running it? It would be a great scandal should I be found out."

"Hide behind a name, Seth. Just do something, man!"

And so it had come to pass. The opening day arrived, Kenneth and I interviewing women who had come calling for work. There would be two types — waitresses and whores — and a man, one who went by the name John Robins, would oversee them all, taking full responsibility for "owning" the club in return for a hefty wage. Despite the nature of the business, I am proud of what Kenneth and I have done. If it means we save only one prostitute from that terrible man's clutches, it will have been worth it.

Tonight...ah, I am looking forward to tonight. Yesterday, a woman had stopped by the club, her head bowed, face partially obscured by the hood of her black cloak. Her eyes darted from side to side as she stood in front of my office desk. She enquired about work, giving her name as Violet, and a spark of recognition flared inside me. I recognised not only her voice but the amethyst ring that glittered on her finger. Violet indeed.

I smiled, allowing her to think she had gulled me, and asked what her friend "Lily" looked like. My suspicions were proved correct when she described the beauty who had long since filled my dreams. Pearl Lewis, a woman I had coveted for the two years since her parents' terrible deaths.

What a debacle that had been. What a tragedy. And, so

rumour had it, Pearl Lewis had vowed to hate me forever, even though, as far as I knew, she had never set eyes on me. I cannot say I blame her. I documented the incident when it happened, but I cannot help but remember it as though it happened only today. While out hunting, one of my employees had accidentally shot her father, and Pearl had apparently voiced her opinion that had I not petitioned that it was accidental, she may not have hated me so vehemently. Her mother, God rest her soul, had been desolate and took her own life shortly after her husband's funeral, leaving Pearl to the care of an elderly aunt and a lifetime of hatred for me.

I took it upon myself to look out for Pearl, asking after her health via people who frequented the same circles as she. She had secluded herself, seemingly shying from any attempt her aunt made to find her a husband, and as I have penned before, I am not upset about that. If she were to marry, I would find myself quite bereft — I have entertained dreams of sweeping her off her feet and having her fall in love with me. A silly notion, I know, but one I cannot seem to rid from my mind.

When "Violet" finished her description of "Lily", I sat for a while in silence, watching her shift from foot to foot. What the devil did they need employment for? And, more to the point, why did they want employment in my club?

"It is hardly the type of venue suited to women of your class, *Frances*."

Her head shot up, her gaze boring into me with such intensity I almost laughed.

"What is it to you why we wish to work here?" she snapped. "I heard employment was on offer and here I am. Are we not suitable for waitress work?"

I fondled my chin, the beginnings of new beard growth rasping against my palm. "I would wager neither of you have the slightest idea of how to serve drinks. After all," I paused and smiled, "you have servants who do such things in your homes."

Her cheeks flared, the red hue prominent as she glared at me, and I stifled the urge to laugh again. This woman, I thought, who stood there thinking she could manage a club full of men who wanted nothing more than to paw her body, was rather deluded.

"We can learn," she said. "And if we do not like it, I know where the door is."

"And what if you are recognised?" I asked, enjoying the ridiculous scenario. "As well as the upper end of the lower class, and also the middle class, there will be men who come here who know you."

She disguised a gasp very well and bunched her fists at her sides. "Face paint. It is marvellous at changing one's features."

"It is, but it will not disguise Lily's hair. We have uniforms but we do not have wigs." I snorted to hide a chuckle.

"Will you agree to us working here or not?" she asked, tapping her foot on the wooden floor.

I nodded, pinching my chin between finger and thumb. "I will, but the moment you are spotted, do not come crying to me. You shall deal with the consequences of your actions, and if you mention that I own this club, no one will believe you. Do you understand what I am saying?"

She nodded, narrowing her eyes as she no doubt weighed up her options. "Yes, I understand."

"Well, then. You will start tomorrow night at nine. Do *not* be late."

She eyed me slyly. "I heard a rumour you have your heart set on Lily."

Her words had caught me off guard, and I wondered what her point was. "I do. I make no secret of it. I am surprised she has not heard these rumours herself."

"Violet" smiled. "Do you realise if she finds out who you are she will scratch out your eyes if her aunt has her way?"

"So I have heard. Although, I doubt very much you will be the one to tell her. I sense you have not told her what you have heard with regards to my feelings towards her."

"I have not." She clasped her fingers together.

"You keeping my feelings a secret is a breach of her trust, is it not? Would a friend not tell her the man she thinks she hates is in love with her?"

Her cheeks flushed. "Yes, I suppose a friend would." She paused, then said, "Do you intend getting to know her tomorrow night?"

What the devil was her game? "I might."

"Then it would serve you well to keep mine and Lily's business here quiet."

What a wily woman. She would keep a secret if I would.

And here I am, writing this before leaving for the club, wondering if Violet and Lily will arrive. What business they have here I do not know, but I am intrigued to find out. What a pleasure it will be to watch Lily weave between the tables, a tray held aloft, her hips swaying. What a pleasure indeed.

* * * *

I am penning this on a sheet of paper, unable to wait until I get home. I must write down my thoughts now before they fade away. Remembering everything is important to me—I am not foolish enough to think Pearl will ever come around to loving me, or even liking me for that matter. Therefore, I have only my dreams, written down so I can read them again and again.

She arrived not a half-hour ago, walking into the club with her chin to chest, her red hair obscuring the perfect features I have branded into my mind. My, she is a beauty, her bone structure like the finest carving, her eyes the colour of summer grass. I watched her from a darkened corner, saw how she hid behind Frances and peered at the empty club, her eyes wide. She bit her lower lip and took everything in—the many tables and chairs that give the appearance this is just a place for men to drink, the bar that stretches from beside the entry door to the far wall, and the door beside me that leads to my office and the upper bedrooms.

Her gaze did not falter as it swept past where I stood. My heart fluttered, beat so damn hard I almost gasped, and I wished things could have been different. Wished she did not hate me. But she does, and there is nothing I can do to change her mind except perhaps to approach her while she works and see if she does, in fact, recognise me. After all, she may well have found out who I am since proclaiming how she feels, sought me out to catch a glimpse of the man who stood up for his employee.

I have often wondered whether her hatred towards me has been exacerbated by her grief. Surely once she emerged from the mourning process she realised it *was* an accident, and that my support for my employee meant he was a good man who did not deserve to take the blame for a crime he did not intend to commit. Still, hate me she does, and there may well be nothing I can do about that now.

I can but try to encourage her to love me.

Another waitress came out of the door opposite me that leads to the women's dressing room, whisking Pearl and Frances away and out of my sight. I stopped myself from following, from walking through that door to seek her out and beg her to give me a chance to explain. She would not listen, I know that, and when I think of all the things that could hurt me, I do believe that would hurt the most. To see derision in her eyes, to know she despises me…no, I cannot bear having the rumours confirmed. Better that I tell myself those snippets of information had been twisted before they arrived to my ear.

I remained in the corner, pulling a chair out and sitting at a table. The barman brought over a whisky at the wave of my hand, and I sipped and waited, sipped and waited. She came through the door a different woman, her face further prettied by rouge, lipstick and a smattering of blue shadow on her eyelids. A wall lamp illuminated her face, shone on her beautiful red hair so the waves almost gleamed, and I longed to run my fingers through it, to feel the silky goodness on my skin. She strode to the bar, and it was as though the face paint and different outfit had altered her into someone quite unlike the person who had entered. That frightened woman had become a bold hussy, and my cock hardened as I stared.

What is she doing here? Why has she come?

I will never know unless I ask, unless I get to know her somehow. If she is unaware of who I am, my task will be easy, and I must pray that this will be so. I cannot contemplate the other scenario.

Men filed in when the doors opened for business and studied her with obvious lechery in their eyes. How I remained seated I do not know, and again another whisky appeared on my table, swallowed in one gulp with the casual wave that I wanted more. One more, that was all. I needed to keep my wits about me.

As she walked the floor, enjoying the attention while bringing ale and spirits to the men sitting at the tables or those lounging against the walls, I rose, unable to stop my mind from conjuring thoughts of her in my bed. I should not look upon her in the same way as the other women, seeing her as someone I can bed if that is what I choose, but God help me, I cannot stop myself. She is like a drug, the mere sight of her luring me into waters I can only drown in.

Listen to me. I sound a pretentious fool, prone to poetic lines that would put me to shame should anyone read my journal. But I cannot help the way she makes me feel. I must go back to the club, take my seat and ensure that no men mistake Pearl for someone she is not. Already I have witnessed them reaching out to touch her, hence me fleeing up here to write frantically while at the same time wishing I had never left. Already I miss being in her presence.

Before I flew up here, Kenneth arrived, eyes growing wide upon spotting Pearl tending to the customers. He found me in the gloom and made straight for me, dragging out a chair and sitting opposite.

"Is that who I think it is?" he asked, jabbing his thumb

over his shoulder.

"It is."

I watched her behind him. She placed down a tankard of ale two tables over and eased out of the reach of grasping fingers, fingers I had the urge to break. If that man touched her he would know what pain was.

"Bejesus." Kenneth sighed. "Fucked if I understand the fairer sex. In all that is sane and right, what the shit is she doing here?" He shook his head, staring at me to catch any change in my expression that meant he needed to intervene in whatever went on behind him. I can read him well, having known him so long.

"I have no idea. Frances applied for them both."

"Frances Wilkins?"

I nodded. "The very same."

"Will wonders never cease, man?"

"Apparently not." I swigged my whisky.

"Will you approach her?" Kenneth glanced back then returned his gaze to me. "She's popular…"

"A little too popular, I feel." I rose and walked through the door to my rear, jealousy eating a hole in my gut, and left Kenneth to keep an eye on the woman I had come to think of as mine.

I went into the washroom situated off the office and leaned against the wall. My breathing came out ragged, as if I had scarpered down Commercial Street in fear of my life. I stared at myself in the mirror above the sink, startled at my flushed cheeks and a lock of black hair that hung limply over my brow. This was not the face of the man I was used to seeing. No, this was a man unsure of himself, at sixes and sevens and unable to control his urges. Thoughts of Pearl flicked through my mind then, and I leaned my head back, closing my eyes to see her better. She stood before me, a smile on her face, her eyes bright, and she leant forward to kiss me.

Perhaps I should not write such detail in my journal, but I will just the same. My cock grew hard at the sight of her, and even though I knew she was not real it did not matter to my body. It reacted as though I truly witnessed her in front of me, and I felt the brush of her hand on mine. Maybe I had become delusional, that seeing her in my establishment, so close and yet so far away, had sent me insane, but I allowed myself that one moment. She caressed my face, the scent of her wafting towards me, and I breathed her in, the aroma of jasmine highly arousing. My balls ached, throbbed with my need for her, and I gave in to their calling before I could change my mind.

Freeing my cock, I fisted it, gave it several short jerks then eased my fist into a longer, slower rhythm. Pearl nestled into me, her body warmth further swelling my cock, and she slipped out her tongue, trailing the tip along my bottom lip. I sucked in a breath, loving the wet heat, the feel of her tongue on my mouth, and flicked my own to brush hers. She touched her lips to mine, plunging her tongue inside, bringing up her hands to twine her fingers in my hair. And I took my chance to do the same to her, gripping her locks and holding her head steady. She pushed her head back, pulled her mouth from mine, and looked up at me with eyes greener than I remembered. God, but she was pretty, and it struck me then that I stared at a face without paint, the face I loved, bare of enhancement and how nature intended.

It was too much, that daydream, and I jerked on my cock, rushing towards a release that never seemed enough, never left me fulfilled. I ejaculated into my palm, the expulsion hot and fast, and sagged, my knees momentarily giving way. With eyes still closed, I watched her retreat, a smile on her face and her finger beckoning me to follow her, to seek her out downstairs.

As I cleaned up, I wondered what she was doing at that very moment. Had she felt any form of connection when I had come, sensed that someone somewhere had seen her every night in his dreams for the past two years and could not for the life of him stop thinking about her?

I doused my face in cold water, the liquid shocking me out

of my dreamlike state, and chastised myself at how fanciful I had become. I was acting like a lovesick fool who believed there was someone out there for everyone, and that the soul-mate I believed her to be would know I existed, feel my love for her. Of course she would not feel it. Nor would she know how obsessed with her I had become.

And she never would if I did not tell her.

And here I am, wasting time up here when I could be down there. But I am afraid—afraid she will reject me before I have the chance to explain, whether it is due to her recognising me or because of my approaching her like a common customer. Yet go down I must, for who knows whether she will be back after tonight?

She may even have already gone.

Chapter Three

November 9th, 1888

The time well past midnight, Pearl was thrilled to the bone with the freedom she felt while rushing from the bar to the tables. Although the men reaching out to touch her skirts were more than a little unsettling at first—frightening, even—she slowly got used to it, telling herself she could manage their attentions for one night. Her emotions were all over the place, though. One minute she felt horrified, the next fascinated. The thought of what would happen if she were found out...being ostracized from society, sent away in shame, married off to a man destined to forever be tainted by a wife who did not know her place. If such a man existed. Who would want to marry her if this came out?

I should have thought this through properly. We should go home. Surely it is nearly morning by now. It seems we have been here all night.

She glanced around the room, noting the air had greyed with curls of pipe smoke. Seeking her friend, intent on telling her they must leave—now—she spotted Frances laughing with a man beside a door she assumed led upstairs. Frances appeared to be enjoying herself quite a lot, as far as Pearl could tell, without the embarrassment Pearl herself was experiencing. This was so wrong, so dreadfully wrong, yet she was glad they had come. The conflicting emotions made her frown.

She sighed. *I entered into this willingly. I knew what the consequences would be.*

Life had been dreary, painful at times when in mourning,

41

and tonight had so far taken her focus off the tedium. Her mind raced with a hundred and one things, more questions as to whether she should be here, whether being so would come back to haunt her later in life. *What if, what if, what if?*

She thrust away the thought of being caught and told herself to enjoy the next few hours, pledging to worry about any consequences later. And what of them anyway? She was destined to be an old maid, forgotten by society once she had reached a certain age, never to be thought of or seen again unless by chance.

"Whisky, little miss," a man said, tugging her skirt.

She looked down at the coarse black fabric of her dress, which scratched her skin, the fibres digging into her waist, then at the hand that clutched it. A work-worn hand, knuckles and finger joints rough. She wondered what he did for a living, whether he was married and if his wife sat at home awaiting his return.

"Certainly," she said with a smile, hiding the pang of guilt that he eyed her with longing. *If he has a wife I feel sorry for her.*

Turning, she moved away, the man only relinquishing his hold on her skirt when the material pulled taut. She glanced back, spied his wink and the lick of his lips, and her stomach tightened as she imagined the thoughts running through his mind. Were all men like this? Whatever station they belonged to? She could not imagine her father behaving this way, or even Luke the carriage driver. No, some men were gentlemen, and this man most certainly was not.

She reached the bar and requested the whisky, wondering how the men paid for what they consumed. Did their membership fee cover liquor? She had so much to learn about life, and the sudden thought that she had been sheltered for far too long struck her with more force than usual. Sighing—had the barman forgotten her request?— she raised herself on tiptoes and lifted one hand to gain his attention. Useless of her to do so really, as he stood at the other end of the bar with his back to her, conversing with a man whose yellowed teeth and unkempt hair made him stand out.

She sighed again and waited until he realised she stood waiting, then took the whisky to the man who had asked for it. As she moved away from him to speak to another fellow who had waved for her to attend to him, another waitress cut her off mid-stride. Pearl eyed the young blonde, wondering what she could want, and the brief thought that she had done something wrong made her stomach roil. Oh, she would only be here for one night, so a mistake did not matter overmuch, but still, she would not want to be seen as a lax employee. She smiled at the woman in the hope it would cease her jagged nerves.

"You're needed in one of the private rooms," the blonde said, her broad London accent rough despite the woman clearly trying to disguise it. "The woman who runs us girls told me to come and find you."

Pearl frowned. She had taken on employment as a waitress, so what she could be needed for puzzled her. "Do they require drinks?" She fisted the fabric of her skirts. Would her nerves ever stop jangling?

"I don't know," the blonde said. "All I know is you're needed, and I'm just doin' what I'm told." She scowled, looked at Pearl as though she did not possess a working brain, and moved to walk away.

Pearl grasped her arm, turning the woman to face her. "But I...I should not need to go upstairs."

"Look, this ain't nothin' to do with me, all right? I just do what I'm asked. Besides, you get paid more for workin' upstairs, if you catch my meanin'. You'd do well to change jobs. I'm lookin' to work up there myself. And with your pretty face, you'll be hard pressed to fight the fellas off." Her smile was one of envy, and she turned away, walking with purpose towards the door Pearl had guessed led upstairs. Once there, she turned and snapped, "Well? You just goin' to stand there starin' all night? Get up these bloody stairs, will you?"

Although startled by the woman's abrasive tone, Pearl did as she was bade. She followed the blonde up a wooden stairway and rounded the newel post at the top to see a landing with several mahogany doors. Her stomach bunched, trepidation making her knees weak and her head light. Low moans issued from behind the doors, and although Pearl had not engaged in such acts, she knew very well what was happening in those rooms. Perhaps the madam occupied a room alone and wanted to interview Pearl about a more active position. Well, she would have to say that was not possible. One night only as a waitress, that was all. She could not return here. Could she?

No, I cannot. I must forget this night and continue with my usual life.

The blonde knocked on a door at the far end of the corridor, glancing at Pearl as she lowered her hand. She whispered, "You ought to make sure you're polite when you go in, otherwise you'll lose your chance of a better job. I can tell just by lookin' at you that you're new to this. Her in there," she jerked her head towards the door, "will want to let you know what's expected of you, see if you're up to the challenge."

Before Pearl could explain that she did not want a new job, a strong, sultry female voice called out that they should enter. With her stomach rolling again, Pearl followed the blonde into the room.

Pearl looked around, squinting to become accustomed to the darkness, illuminated by only one candle. Its light danced in the breeze their entrance created. A black-haired woman sat on a velvet chair in the far corner beside the bed. A wispy black dressing gown with frills down the front did little to hide her naked body beneath. Pearl snatched in a quick breath, startled that the madam sat there with her charms on show as though it mattered not one bit. How wonderful it would be, to be so at ease with one's body like that. Pearl's cheeks grew hot, and she kept her focus on the madam's face to save herself from being embarrassed further.

"You may leave us," the madam said, nodding to the blonde. She twirled one finger in the air, obviously impatient to move on with the meeting. "Return to your room. I am sure a customer will join you soon."

As the blonde left, the door snicking quietly closed behind her, Pearl laced her fingers to occupy them. Her thoughts raced, her legs weakening. She wanted to turn and run out of this room, out of this place and into the safety of the carriage.

"Sit," the madam said, pointing to a chair in the opposite corner beside the door.

Pearl opened her mouth to protest. She did not want to sit, did not want to be in a semi-dark room where the drapes closed out the night and the air smelt of something faintly musty. She was out of her depth, scared to stay yet scared to disobey the woman.

What a ridiculous situation to have found herself in. She did not belong here, had known that from the moment she had walked into the club earlier, but here she was, moving towards the chair and sitting on it.

The window was between the two chairs, giving Pearl some distance so she felt safe enough, given that the door was only feet away. Something about the madam's demeanour sparked fear inside her. The bed sitting in the other corner did too, and she sat tensely, ready to spring out of her seat if the need arose.

"You are frightened," the madam stated, rising to stand in front of Pearl.

Her gown barely covered her full, heavy breasts. Her nipples were exposed, the candlelight just bright enough to show their hardness, the puckered outer circles. The lack of underwear drew Pearl's attention to the madam's hairy nest, and her heart thundered as she acknowledged the shocking foreignness of this moment. She lowered her head, stared at the expensive-looking carpet, her blush getting hotter by the second.

"There is no need to be scared. I only wish for you to watch."

Watch? Watch what? Dear God, what am I doing here? Why did I ever agree to come?

Pearl lifted her head, opening her mouth to voice those very thoughts, but the madam spoke first.

"I am fully aware you do not wish to engage in anything more than waitressing, but I sense a curiosity in you. Am I correct?"

Pearl was reticent to admit such a thing, but her head betrayed her, and she nodded in answer.

"Just as I thought. It would not hurt to watch, hmm? Just to see if your curiosity can be satisfied. There would be no harm." She laughed, a light tinkle that went some way to calming Pearl. "You could see what this is all about then leave… Or it may well make you want to join us up here instead of working downstairs."

Pearl jerked her head up. "But I am here for only one night. I just wanted to see—"

"Yes, I understand. Then see you will. Just sit. Watch. If it becomes too much…well, then you will know you are not suited to this profession."

"I am not suited, I know that. I—"

"Then why the devil are you here, hmm? Curiosity is not enough to risk your reputation. There must be some other reason. Perhaps you burn to know what this is all about. Perhaps there is a woman inside you who is dying to come out, yet this world in which we live will not allow it."

How does she know? Am I so easily read?

She stared at the madam, searching for a sign that would tell her what she longed to know. Was she secretly yearning to sell her body, was that it? Or was it how she had initially thought, that she just wanted to see, to have a taste of something she otherwise would never sample? She preferred the latter explanation, and asked herself if she could indeed watch without running out of the room shocked to her toes. Would seeing a man rutting with a woman scar her for life or make her want to experience some of the same?

She did not know, but something pinned her bottom to the seat and refused to make her legs work in order for her to leave the room. No one knew she was up here except the madam and the blonde. Frances need never know, and Pearl would have a secret all her own to keep for the rest of her life.

I will stay and watch. Like she said, if it is not to my liking, I can leave.

She nodded at the madam and settled back in her chair, hands clasped in her lap to keep them from shaking. The black-haired woman nodded back and disappeared out the door, returning so quickly with a man in tow that Pearl had no time to digest her decision.

Oh, my God. He is gentry…

She took him in from head to foot, his well-kept dark hair and beard, his fine clothing. She did not recognise him, but his bearing alone marked him as a man who came from the upper classes. She wondered whether he had a wife, children, but the thought was stripped from her mind along with the jacket and shirt the madam swiftly removed from his body.

Pearl stifled a gasp as the man turned to look at her, bare-chested, a smattering of hair running down the centre. His smile, one of amusement, made her blush harder. Unable to turn away from eyes that sparkled by the light of the candle, Pearl stared, admitting that his beauty far outweighed her fear. She would stay seated for as long as she could. She did not question why, did not want to entertain the idea that she was a dirty woman. Not yet.

The madam drew him to the bed and stood before him, deftly taking off his lower garments. His excitement was revealed, long, wide and rigid, and Pearl could not take her gaze from it. Lord, it stood proudly jutting from his body, made her itch to know what it felt like, and she sucked in a breath to still her fast-beating heart.

Naked, he turned to face Pearl, as if presenting himself for her inspection. The candlelight lit one side of him, casting the other into shadow, and the sight was more than appealing. She eyed the way his hip bones tapered, disappearing into a riot of curls surrounding the base of his turgid length. The way those curls changed to straighter ones on his thighs. He was breathtaking, possibly more so because he was the first man she had seen without clothing. Fascinated, she studied him some more and imagined how his skin would feel compared to hers. It would be rougher, she wagered, what with those hairs, and a delicious thrill erupted between her legs.

That brought her up short. She was excited when she should have been horrified. What was wrong with her? She moved to rise, but the man turned away and approached the madam, taking away Pearl's idea of leaving the room.

Just a little longer. It will not hurt to stay for a moment more, to see what will happen next.

He peeled the nightgown from the madam's shoulders, letting the garment fall to the floor. She smiled up at him as though she loved him dearly, all traces of her somewhat hard personality of before vanishing.

She is able to play a part, to change at will.

This aspect mesmerised her, and she knew then that her curiosity would keep her pinned to the seat. Squeezing her hands together, she took in a long, quiet breath.

The madam smiled at him then reached up to place her hands on his shoulders. "Lick my cunt," she said, pushing him down to his knees.

Pearl's heart raced at the woman's use of such a word. Would she ever be able to utter the same? She was not sure she could, but rolled the word around in her mind anyway, testing the sound of it as it echoed. Deciding she liked it, she watched as the madam parted her legs, baring her folds for his inspection. He spread her slit open and gazed at the dark pink flesh. His hard length strained as he took in the glistening hairs, the engorged bud at the apex. Pearl stared open-mouthed, entranced at the view and that the woman had no air of embarrassment about her at all. She was comfortable with her body, that much was evident, and seemed to thrive on being on show like this. Her smile proved it, as did the way she raised her hands from her sides to clasp the sides of his head.

"I *said*, lick my cunt."

She brought his head down and canted her hips, offering herself to him. He breathed in deeply, closed his eyes, and his tongue snaked out of his mouth to slide from her base to her hood. His low "mmmm" of appreciation gave Pearl a glimpse into how this act made a man feel, how he enjoyed what he was doing. Could she do that? Could she allow a man to lick her there? She did not know, but perhaps one day, if she was lucky enough to have a man call to court her, she could engage in an act just like this.

The man lapped, the sound of his tongue against the woman's juices loud in the room. It joined the madam's frantic breathing, and Pearl shifted her gaze from what the man was to doing to the woman's face. She had closed her eyes, and Pearl detected a faint blush on her cheeks. The madam licked her lips, possibly in time with the man's strokes, and a stuttered groan erupted from her mouth, as though she was in pain.

"Oh, that feels wonderful," the madam breathed. "Harder. Lick me harder."

So it did not hurt, then. The groan was undoubtedly one of pleasure. Pearl wiggled in her seat, stifling a groan of her own. This…this scene before her was something she had never expected to witness, and had Frances or Elizabeth asked her if she would contemplate being a spectator she would have shot them a scathing glance and a few harsh words. Yet here she was, in a place she had never thought she would be, with people she had never thought she would meet. How odd that her life had changed so drastically in such a short space of time.

The madam's groans grew more frequent, lasted longer,

and her grip tightened on the man's hair. She fisted it, held him closer, and circled her hips against his face. Pearl could only imagine the pleasure the woman felt. She had been touched there only by her own fingers, and a tongue was much softer…

Abandoning his licking, the man sucked her bud into his mouth, and he kissed her folds like he would a mouth. Pearl leant forward a little to get a better look, then sat back quickly when she realised what she had done. Although she was curious, she did not want the madam to know.

The woman stared down at him. "Stop that. Lick it again now. Hard, fast."

He obeyed and reared back a little, giving Pearl the view of how he expertly attended to the woman. He swirled his tongue around her bud, up and down her slit, and, good Lord, it seemed he must have pushed his tongue inside her hole as it disappeared from view. Pearl needed some air. The room had become altogether too stuffy, and the scent she had detected earlier upon entrance was stronger now.

It must be the smell of the woman.

The madam keened, her hips jolting rapidly in front of the man's face, his mouth and nose vanishing in the surrounding hairs. Pearl watched in fascination as desire peaked for the woman. She juddered, shrieked out, and Pearl imagined the bliss the madam felt was more than she herself had ever experienced when she had touched herself.

"Enough!" the woman said, stepping back and beckoning for him to stand. "You know what I want now."

The man spun the madam around so she faced the bed. He pressed a splayed hand to the top of her back so she bent over, hands braced on the bed for support. With a swift movement, he eased one knee between her legs and in no time her legs stood apart, bottom tilted upward. The curve of her buttocks did not give beneath the man's touch as he smoothed his palms over them. The woman had not an inch of spare flesh on her body. He caressed her back with slow, languid strokes, massaging her shoulders each time he reached them. A smile curved his mouth, and he glanced sideways at Pearl, one eyebrow raised.

A silent question as to whether she liked what she saw.

She admitted she did, although it was wrong. So very wrong.

Still looking at Pearl, he took himself in hand and guided his hardness between the madam's legs. By God, he was entering her, pushing his length inside until it disappeared from view. A thrill of excitement bloomed in Pearl's slit, much stronger than she had ever experienced from her fingers. Wetness seeped out of her folds, bringing with it the need to touch herself to ease the incessant beat that throbbed there. Oh, this was so wrong, yet she could not bring herself to leave the room.

Just a little while longer…

The man pulled out until only his tip remained inside, then shoved back in with such a hard thrust that Pearl gasped. She blushed at her outburst, at the sidelong look the man gave her, his smile wider now. He brushed his hands up the woman's sides and fondled her breasts, his fingers working quickly over her nipples as he began moving in and out of her. He gained a fast pace, his leg muscles standing out boldly every time he surged, the cheek of his bottom dipping at the same time.

"Fuck my cunt," the madam said, her breaths rapid. "Yes, fuck my cunt!"

The words stunned Pearl into standing. Never had she heard anyone use them before tonight, and despite the shock, she remained where she was, feet seemingly glued to the carpet. Those words, so bad, so naughty, inspired a flood of cream to seep out of her slit. She squirmed in place, the liquid at the tops of her inner thighs making her legs glide. And, God, the fierce throbbing between her legs intensified to a level where she knew she would have to either leave the room or find an obscure way to assuage the need raging there. Her nub swelled, its expansion swift, sudden, and it felt as though it might burst if she did not touch herself soon.

No, I cannot do that. Not here. Not with them in the room.

She stared at the couple. The man thrust harder, faster, sweat breaking out on his temple, a droplet dribbling down his cheek. He continued to play with her breasts, his fingers working so quickly their movement became a blur. With hot cheeks and a rampant need to have her desires fulfilled, Pearl could do nothing but witness the man buck and jerk. His head snapped back, and he stared at the ceiling, neck tendons corded. He clenched his teeth, took his hands from her breasts and placed one on her shoulder. The other he drew out to his side, then brought it crashing down on her outer thigh. The smack gave Pearl a huge start, shocked her that he had struck a woman in such a way, yet at the same time she was curious as to how it felt. The madam groaned, one of pleasure not pain, and released a feral growl.

"Do it again. Oh, God, yes, do it again. I love it. Fuck my cunt and slap me. I love it!"

Her language burst the build-up of excitement in Pearl's folds. It spread without her touch, seeping through to her core until her torso shuddered and she let out a low moan. The man thrust even faster. His groan joined hers and the madam's as he slapped her thigh again.

Shame spread through Pearl, guilt joining it for the ride, and the sudden realisation of what she had witnessed, how her body had reacted, had her running from the room and slamming the door behind her.

Oh, God. Oh, my good God…

Breathless, she blindly raced down the stairs, the moans and groans from behind the doors mocking sounds that followed her into the club. Glancing about, she made herself slow down and entered the changing room in order to make sense of her body and mind's reaction upstairs.

Did this mean she was a filthy woman? That she had enjoyed watching two people in an intimate act surely meant she would go straight to hell. Confused and a little frightened, she went to the dressing table and dipped a handkerchief into a water bowl there. She dabbed the coolness on her temples, mindful that she wore face paint, and breathed out slowly. Her nub still ached, her folds were still slick with juices from her enjoyment, and the heat of more shame burned her cheeks.

The door opened, and she whirled to face who had come in. Frances closed the door and stared at her, head cocked, eyes narrowed. "Are you all right? I saw you dash through the club. Did a customer do something he should not?"

So Frances had not seen where Pearl had been.

"Something like that. I just needed a little time alone." *I needed to get away from this madness, but it is still here. I am still here.*

"Oh, so long as you are not upset. I thought you were."

"No, no. Not upset." *Just angry with myself. My body. Of being so weak-willed I allowed myself to come here. Curiosity or not, that is no excuse to have agreed to this night.*

"Well then. I shall return to my duties." Frances giggled and left the room.

Left Pearl to contemplate what on earth she had done.

53

Chapter Four

November 9th, 1888

Back in the main room, a flustered Pearl laid one hand on the bar, the other down by her side holding a tray. A waft of air from movement beside her chilled her exposed chest, and she turned to her left to see who was there. A man, black cloak about his shoulders and a top hat upon his head, scowled at her as though she were dirt beneath his highly polished shoes. Tiny balls of rain spattered the cloak, some beginning to seep into the fabric from the warmth in the club. She asked herself if he had come in only to shelter from the bad weather or if… He did not look the kind to… She held back a laugh. What did *she* know about kinds?

He stared at her, his gaze hard, as though it could penetrate into her soul. She shivered. An air of menace came off him, mixed with the dirty aroma of rain and a pomade she had never smelt before. Pearl drew her shoulder away from him.

He stood side-on to the bar, one hand placed on top of it, gloved fingers splayed. Leaning forward a touch, he kept her spellbound with his coal-black eyes. His square jawline bled into his chin as though it were one smooth slice of bone, and his flat face made him appear foreign. Uneasy, Pearl stepped away, her hip banging into someone on her right. The man's top lip retracted, showing perfect white teeth, their size too small to belong to an adult, as though those from his infancy had refused to fall out.

"Bitch."

Had he said that? Had that word, that whisper, really

been uttered, or had she imagined it, the sound really something else—the shift of a foot or the brush of one arm against another? She widened her eyes, words failing her, clogging her throat. Pearl turned her head to avoid looking into those piercing eyes that made dread churn in her belly.

I am out of my depth. I should never have come.

"You are filthy," came that voice again, abrading her sensitivities and bringing tears to her eyes. "A certain man would think nothing of slicing you from neck to pelvis and showing the world the badness inside you."

Oh, God. Does he know what I did upstairs?

His breath met her, the scent of it sour and vinegary, and despite her desire to run in fear, she straightened her spine and whirled to face him.

"Do not presume to know who I am," she said, narrowing her eyes in the hope she would appear fiercer than she felt. "And speaking of that man…that monster, with such pleasure in your tone is revolting."

Her heart pounded too hard, too fast, and she inhaled through her nose to calm it. A hot blush warmed her cheeks until they itched, but she resisted lifting her hand to scratch them. The man eyed her with disdain, that lip curled back again, his nostrils flared in an unsightly manner. He raised one hand, but Pearl refused to flinch. If he intended to strike her she would take the abuse, sure that someone would come to her aid. Instead, he took his hat brim between finger and thumb and lifted it a little from his head.

"I do not presume," he said, voice hard and airy at the same time, as though he struggled to breathe due to his surprise—or was it anger?—at her outburst. "I know who and what you are. Your being here tells me quite plainly what you will be doing until the early hours. The stink of you tells me you have indulged in carnal pleasures."

Indignant at his presumption, yet knowing he had made a valid point with his statement, Pearl bristled and bit back a retort. She would not win an argument with this man—a man who was quite clearly looking for one. Squaring her shoulders, she stared into his sinister eyes and held his gaze, wanting to show him she was unafraid, even though she quivered inside and wished he would leave.

"I would hope," said a man behind her, "that your somewhat threatening words were spoken in jest, sir."

The man shifted his eyes to look over her shoulder, and he doffed his hat again. The meanness vanished from his eyes, replaced with what Pearl assumed was respect. He smiled, a grin of teeth clamped together, one that did not reach his eyes, and backed towards the door. Gripping his cloak in one hand beneath his chin, he gave Pearl one last dark look then turned away, striding out the door.

Soft breaths caressed her shoulder, and Pearl, unsteady on her feet and more than a little perturbed by the altercation, spun to face her rescuer. He smiled, a lock of black hair hanging between his eyes, his clean-shaven face at odds with what she was used to seeing, men with full beards or moustaches.

Her breath caught in her throat as she opened her mouth to thank him, but she closed her lips for fear a squeak would emerge instead of her gratitude. He regarded her with mid-blue eyes, flecks of navy spiking out from their black centres, and smiled wider, a twitch flicking at one corner of his mouth.

"I am dreadfully sorry about that man." He glanced at the door then back at her. "Some men do not know how to behave around a lady."

He held out a hand and Pearl clasped it. Heat from his palm warmed her skin and a flush spread on her face to join the heat of anger already there. Bending his head, his gaze still on her face, this fellow, this man who had no business making her knees weak and her stomach tighten, pressed his lips to the back of her hand.

Good God above, Pearl felt faint. She gripped the tray in her other hand and stumbled backward a bit. He straightened, his hold on her fingers tightening to help steady her. She smiled and blushed hotter, dipping her head to show him her thanks.

"What is your name?" he asked, releasing her hand and leaning one elbow on the bar.

The feeling of his kiss still lingered on her hand. Branded on her skin. "P—Lily." Gosh, would he stop looking at her like that? As though he loved the sight of her? She swallowed and tried to look away, wanting to seek out Frances so she could break free of this hold he appeared to have on her.

"Lily. That *is* lovely. My name is… Are you all right?" He cocked his head.

"Yes, thank you. That man, he… I do not know him. He—"

"Is a pompous ass." His lips stretched wider.

"Well, yes, I suppose he is." *I think you are truly beautiful.*

Pearl smiled, took the whisky from the barman, and walked away on unsteady legs. She continued to work, conscious of her rescuer watching her every move. His attention delighted her, but at the same time she was at a loss as to how to deal with the emotions his study wrought. She imagined him taking her, making her a true woman, him becoming the man she usually had these private fancies about. Was it wrong, this secret imagining, when he stood only feet away?

After what could have been an hour, or maybe even two of avoiding being close to him, Pearl approached the bar with an order for the rowdy gentlemen at table eight. She stood beside the man, his presence making her lightheaded and bringing a curiously heavy beat between her legs.

"Is this your first night?" He glanced away for a moment, holding one finger up to the barman as he approached. "Drinks for table eight. Lily is busy at present."

The barman obeyed, pouring quickly and leaving the bar to deliver the drinks himself. Was this man beside her the owner of the club? Or just someone people obeyed, someone whose status in society she was as yet unaware? That would not be surprising, considering she rarely ventured from the house.

The man faced her again, his strong jawline showing the first signs of stubble—tiny black dots just beneath the skin—his cheekbones high, flushed from liquor, perhaps? He was everything she had imagined a suitor to be in the lonely nights she had spent in her room.

How she longed for a normal life, one where, after dinner, the family congregated in one room, a fire and gaslights burning, the household engaging in conversation until time for bed. Instead, she spent her evenings in her bedroom and her aunt in hers, the air cold in winter and her boredom level reaching its peak. Was that how it would always be? Would she ever meet a man who would take her away from it all?

She felt the need to say something, the space of time between his last words and her staring at him too long to be proper. Pearl opened her mouth, ready to tell him she had work to do, but he got there first.

"I realise you have work to do, but can I just be permitted to say…you do not look as though you belong here. In fact, I know you do not belong here."

Pearl's stomach contracted, and she glanced around, frightened, feeling caged. Did he know her and she not know him? *Oh, God, please do not let that be so.* "I…I am here only for one night. I really should leave now. I should go home. It must be nearly morning."

His smile lit up his face and weakened her knees. "I am sure you should. But do you want to, Pearl?"

Pearl? She sucked in a breath. Her legs softened and she dropped the tray, grabbing the bar to steady herself. Men turned to look at her, and she flushed at having caused a scene, the clatter of the tray obscenely loud. She'd known something like this would happen and should have trusted her inner voice. Should never have come here. *Oh, dear Lord. I am undone.*

Frantic, heart throbbing painfully, she whirled away from him in search of Frances, who wove around the tables allowing her bottom to be spanked. Shock and the reality of what they were doing slammed Pearl. What had they been thinking? If she left now, perhaps she could avoid a scandal. Maybe this beautiful man would refrain from letting her secret out.

He clamped his hand on to her upper arm from behind, and she stiffened, wishing him to remove it but at the same time wanting his touch. He brought sensations she had never experienced before and a longing that frightened her with its ferocity. He was a stranger, for goodness' sake, and she was in a place she should never have been. He had to remove his hand before she turned towards him and begged him for more of the same.

What was the matter with her?

She yanked her arm away and started towards Frances, but he grabbed her again and pulled her back against him. Oh Lord, her heart beat faster and that soft place between her legs moistened. Shame filled her, bringing a hot blush to her cheeks she was powerless to stop. His scent swirled around her — tangy and sharp — and the heat from his chest seeping into her back dampened her folds further. She was wretched. A filthy, wretched woman no better than those she thought she could pretend to be.

His breath caressed her neck, bringing on a shiver that hardened her nipples. She supposed this was real desire, an emotion she had only previously enjoyed in its infancy. Nothing like this raging, delightfully sinful heat that spread through her body and rendered her weak.

"Do not be alarmed," he whispered, his voice so soft she wanted to listen to it all night. "I will not reveal your secret."

A little relief came then, but thoughts of whether he spoke the truth ran through her mind. "How…how do you know my name?" She held her breath in readiness for his answer.

"I have known who you are for the longest time. I had hoped to call but I did not feel I would be welcome."

What did he mean? Was he of the lower classes? He did not appear so, his clothing impeccable and his manner faultless. It was not surprising she had not seen him before, cloistered as she was in a house, a life that closed her off — that and her inability to push herself out into the world.

"I do not know you. I should not be here. Please, let me go. I need to leave." Much as she wanted to stay, to be close to him, the fear of being found out proved stronger. "I will pay you to ensure your silence. Please, I—"

"You may pay for my silence by allowing me to visit you at your home."

His voice…oh, it melted every one of her bones, yet also scared her. She had been a fool to think she was ready for marriage, for if this was desire, love, she was drowning in a sea of uncertainty. Did everyone feel like this? In her youth she had heard women talking with her mother, moaning that their husbands wanted to "paw" them every night. Did they not feel how she did now, willing to give their men everything they desired just to experience that heady rush? And his request to visit her. Should she allow that?

"I…yes. You may visit me." *Dear God, what have I said?*

"It is nearly morning, and you will need sleep. Would later this evening be acceptable?" His breath whispered across her neck and collarbone, wetting her folds some more.

"Yes, yes that will be fine."

She pulled away and dashed towards the women's changing room, pushing through the door with a breathless grunt. Panicked, she yanked off the serving dress, glancing about, trying to recall where she had placed her own. Her mind had seemingly filled with air, yet at the same time was filled with questions.

The door opened, and Pearl shrieked, holding the dress up to cover herself as best she could. The man stood in the doorway, most improper, and stared her up and down. She cringed at the thought of men in the club seeing her this way.

"Oh, I do beg your pardon." He averted his gaze, somewhat reluctantly Pearl felt, and stared at the back wall as he closed the door. "I came to ask if I would be staying to dinner or whether it will be just an evening of conversation."

Heat blazed in her face. Pearl clutched the dress in her fists, aware that too much of her was still exposed. He would have seen her underclothes, her bare legs… Dinner. Could she eat with him? "I…I do not mind. You choose." *Please, just go. Please, just stay.*

"Dinner it is, then. Again, my apologies for bursting in here like that. I am not usually so rude. You…you have addled my senses." He opened the door again, easing out through the slight gap, gaze on her face until the door clicked shut.

Addled his senses? What does he mean?

Pearl staggered towards a table holding face paint and seized its edge. Her fingers jostled a lidless pot of powder, which toppled on to its side, the contents spilling. She berated herself for her clumsiness and took a moment to steady her nerves. She had worked a full night here and gained a dinner guest, a man who had turned her whole world upside down.

She no longer knew herself. So many changes had occurred in the last ten minutes, a swift quirk of fate she had not expected and one she did not know how to control. This…this euphoria that enveloped her now, tinged with fear and longing and shameful desire, made her head reel.

She had to leave. She had to dress and tell Frances it was time to go home.

Finding her dress, she folded the other and placed it on a wooden chair. After donning her own, she gave herself a long, hard look in the mirror. Dark rings had formed under her eyes, and her cheeks were so red she scolded herself for looking so wretched. With no time to think about scrubbing her face clean, she pushed through into the bar area, catching Frances's attention.

Frances rushed over. "Is it time to leave?"

"It must be, Frances. Besides," Pearl glanced around nervously then lowered her voice to an urgent whisper, "I have been recognised." She peered over Frances's shoulder, ignoring her friend's look of utter shock. The man had gone, and a huge sense of disappointment made her want to cry.

"Oh, my goodness." Frances held one hand to her chest. "Yes. We must leave. I will be out in a moment." Frances moved to enter the women's room.

Pearl stopped her. "I am going to wait outside. It is too hot in here. I need to get out." The air was cloying, too close. She couldn't breathe.

"You should not go out there alone. These men," she swept her hand up as though to encompass the room, "they may follow. It is not safe, Lily."

Pearl smiled. A good friend, Frances maintained their secret in the earshot of others. "I will go directly to the carriage. I feel a faint coming on. I *have* to get out."

"Promise you will do just that. In the carriage. You *must* stay there. Luke will be waiting." Frances squeezed Pearl's wrist, then disappeared through the doorway, her skirts rustling.

Without waiting to collect her payment for the night's work, Pearl left the building, rushing out to a still-dark street. She looked from left to right, then behind her to ensure no one had followed. Quickly, she dashed into the alley beside the club, her heart beating too fast and her legs weakening from her boldness at being out alone in such an area. This whole evening had been full of madness!

She ran down the alley, turning into the court where Luke had been instructed to wait. It was difficult to see in the gloom, and she scanned the area, noting three carriages, the horses stomping the cobbles at her approach. Saddened that the beasts had not been stabled, she bit back a whispered curse.

Luke's carriage was not there.

No.

Pearl stepped up to each carriage in turn, hoping to recognise the one that had brought them to this place, her mind screaming that Luke could not have abandoned them.

He was supposed to sleep in the carriage. Supposed to wait!

Scared beyond measure, frantic with worry about how they would get home, and the more sinister fear about being in Whitechapel at all, Pearl dashed out of the court and back down the alley. She would go inside and alert Frances. Yes, that was what she would do. Perhaps they could procure a ride home from...who? They could not trust anyone here.

Oh my God, we have been such fools. Such silly little girls.

Pearl blundered out of the alley, smacking straight into a broad, cloaked chest. She shrieked, looking up into the eyes of the man who had been so coarse inside the club earlier. He stared down at her, and she made out dark stains on his face. The stink of copper radiated from him.

His mouth broke out into a terrible smile. "Ah, we meet again, harlot." He lifted one gloved hand, gripping her arm, his other hidden inside his cloak. Did he have a weapon in there?

"Please remove your hand." Pearl had never been so frightened in her life. The tremble in her voice showed her vulnerability and inability to deal with this situation. This man overrode any fear she had of her nighttime activity becoming public knowledge. If he did not let her go...

His shadowed lips closed and, white eyes peeking through the darkness, he regarded her as though she were beneath him. "You are lucky my night's work is done, that I am tired." He drew his hand out of his cloak and held it up.

Something solid and round sat in his palm, the foul odour stronger now, and from the light of a street gas lamp, Pearl saw that whatever he held was wet. He squeezed her arm painfully tight, and she swore her heart stopped for more than three beats. Panic seized her, but the courage to shove him off and run battled for prominence.

Pearl screamed.

The man sprang back, releasing her arm, and scowled before running down the street. She stood for a second or two watching him go, then jumped at the sound of the gentleman's club door banging open and hitting the outer wall. Pearl cried out again, the ordeal too much, and she whirled, once again smacking into a man's chest.

Unable to take any more, Pearl fainted.

Chapter Five

The Diary of Seth Adams

November 9th, 1888

I had retreated to my office once I had recovered enough to walk through the club without anyone knowing my cock was hard to bursting. Seeing Pearl in a state of undress had not been something I had expected — yet. Barely a moment had passed between her leaving my side and entering the women's room, and I surmised she must have been in a desperate hurry to leave the premises for her to have stripped off her dress by the time I walked in. I should have knocked and I cursed myself for not doing so, yet I would be a liar if I said I did not enjoy what I saw.

As she stood there clutching that dress to her breasts, the swells poking above her under-clothes, I had the urge to take her in my arms and declare my love for her. However, propriety allowed no such thing, so I shifted my gaze to the rear wall — such unsightly viewing compared to her! — and hoped that she would forgive my *faux pas*.

I should have left the room immediately, but of course I stayed, like a limpet clinging to a rock, unable to remove myself from her presence. She held me in place, the very air about her charged with something I had never encountered before. What was that? Fear? Longing? I was not sure but hoped for the latter. Although Pearl is clearly a woman brought up in the correct way, I could not help but notice that the unease with which she should have acted was not present. Yes, she was a little afraid and embarrassed, but no, not as much as she should have been. Far from making me think she was indeed the loose woman she had wanted to be, it gave her an air of vulnerability, but at the same time I sensed a red-hot woman beneath the innocent veneer.

I smelt the red-hot woman.

Once in my office, I sat at my desk to write this. How could I not? My thoughts needed to be placed on paper, to leave my head so I had room to sift through our delightful meeting later, at leisure.

I will admit to feeling intense anger at the crass fellow who had spoken to Pearl in such an awful manner. I did not want him near her, breathing the same air, feeling the heat of her skin when he came too close. I have never seen him before, and his bearing showed him as someone who was used to getting his way. He does not frequent my circles, yet he certainly comes from gentry. Although I have never heard a gentleman of good repute speak to a lady—even a woman below his class—in that fashion. Perhaps I have been shielded, am naïve, but I would hate to hear such nasty words again directed at the gentler sex. That they had been directed at Pearl was a rather large mistake on his part, and I will never forget his face. Should I see him again, I can imagine having a few well chosen words to say to him. He is not welcome in the club.

After he had left and Pearl had agreed the man to be a pompous ass, she had looked at me with what I fancied was desire. I cannot be sure, and perhaps that was just my wishful thinking, but by God I wanted to take her in my arms and kiss those pretty lips. Being so close to her had proved a bind, for I could not touch her in the way my hands itched to caress. And my loins be damned! They betrayed me, my cock growing so hard it brought not only raging desire but sweet pain, one I wished her to take away with her mouth, her hands, her...

I am wretched to think of her this way, to be so bold as to write down such feelings, but I cannot help how she makes me feel. It is as though she has bewitched me, this woman

I have longed to become close to for so long. Should she discover who I am — and I am not fool enough to think that she will not — she will not want me anywhere near. This knowledge saddens me more than anything. I do not think I can live without her now that I have spoken to her, heard that beautiful voice and sensed that she has emotions with regard to me that she cannot explain.

I had watched her for hours, the sway of her hips, the way she smiled at the men. Jealousy had churned in my gut at that — I wanted those smiles only for me. As she worked, I racked my mind for some way to meet with her again after this night, to have her see that I am not the Seth Adams she thinks she knows. And for my sins, I came up with the perhaps despicable idea of letting her know I *knew* she should not be in the club. It was ungentlemanly of me, I am fully aware of that, but what other recourse did I have? If she left the club without my having tried to engage her in further conversation, securing a second meeting, I would have hated myself even more than I did my duplicity. And it was for love that I did this thing, this act.

When she had stood beside me once more after avoiding my gaze the entire night, and looked at me sidelong, her lashes obscuring her delightful green eyes, I knew that she welcomed my attention. My plan tumbled from my lips before I could stop it, and her sharp intake of breath at my mention of her name made me feel all kinds of devil. Yet I pressed on, securing a visit with her, my pleasure at having done so shadowing the guilt.

And then I had stumbled into the women's room, fleeing upstairs afterward with a burning cock and pulsating bollocks, my intent to assuage the need there so I could rid myself of desire and pen my diary.

* * * *

I am writing this now in a hansom, on my way to Pearl's for dinner. Events occurred that prevented me writing further in my office earlier, and I did not assuage that need of which I last wrote. I rushed to the window, glancing down into the street. There she was, the beautiful Pearl, out on the cobbles with who appeared to be that dratted fellow. Anger that I had left her in the club without ensuring her safe passage gripped me. As did the sight that she was out there without Frances, and also that the fellow had clearly been waiting for Pearl to leave the club so he could waylay her. In my haste to get out on to the street, I caught my foot on a table leg and went sprawling forward, landing on my knees below the second window.

Frantic, I grasped the sill and hauled myself up, glancing out once again. The man had gripped Pearl's arm in my sojourn to the floor and held something up in one hand. Pearl's scream spirited me away from the window and down the stairs, into a club of men oblivious to the deviousness occurring outside. I flung open the club door, rushing out on to the cobbles as though my very life depended on it. Pearl spun to face me, crashing into my chest, and as she fainted, I closed my arms around her and held her tight. I looked up, a fire in my belly to find that man and beat him to within an inch of his life, but he was too far away. He rounded a far corner, his flapping cape the last I saw of him.

With Pearl my main concern, I lifted her into my arms, her body limp. The club door swung open, and I turned to see Frances on the threshold, her mouth open, face pinched in shock.

"What the devil?" She strode towards me with a bravado I had no doubt was not false. "What are you doing?" She stood before me, delicate hands on hips, a scowl marring her pretty features.

"She fainted. A man of questionable decency had accosted her. I witnessed them from my window." I glanced to the upper windows. "I might ask why you allowed her to venture out here alone. And your accusatory tone does not sit well with me."

"I do not care what it sits with." She narrowed her blazing

eyes. "Unhand her immediately."

I laughed softly, knowing I risked maddening her further. "While she is in such a state? She will not be able to stand, and you," I eyed her small frame, "would not be able to carry her."

Frances huffed out an indignant breath, and her mouth worked with no sound.

"Where is your carriage?" I demanded, the time for games passing with my sudden thought that Pearl should have awoken by now.

"In the yard." Frances pointed to the alley.

"And you have a driver waiting?"

"Why, of course! Do you think us dense?" She strode down the alley, looking back once to ensure I followed.

I did, loving the feel of Pearl so close to me but feeling horrid for revelling in such a thing, at such a time. In the yard, I followed Frances to its centre and matched her glances around the space. "Well? Which one is it?"

She turned to face me, her features in shadow, the sky still not ready to allow the sun to rise. "It is not here."

"I beg your pardon?" I was not sure I had heard her correctly. Surely she had not said —

"It is not here. My driver has gone." She moved forward, placing a hand on Pearl's brow and looking up at me. "Whatever will we do?" Her voice held a hint of alarm and despair.

"I will take you both home. Come." I walked towards my carriage, settling Pearl inside so she reclined across one seat. "Get in," I told Frances, my anger towards her seeping into my tone. How could she have hired such an unreliable driver? What had she been thinking?

Frances, head bowed, climbed aboard and sat on the seat opposite Pearl. I took a blanket, a little damp from the night air, out of the driver's seat that also acted as storage, and handed it to Frances.

"Let me know if she wakes and I will stop." I closed the door, angry at Frances for suggesting this ridiculous escapade to one such as Pearl, an obviously naïve woman who had no cause to imagine their night would have ended this way.

As I boarded the carriage and headed towards Frances's estate, I mulled over the recent events and waited for Frances's knock to tell me Pearl had roused. No knock came, and I hid the disappointment with worry over why Pearl had not woken yet. Had the fellow given her something? Done something to make her sleep this way?

If it was the last thing I did, I would ensure that man paid for what he had done.

After dropping Frances at her home, I continued on to Pearl's, wondering what I would do if she was still asleep by the time we arrived. It did not take a clever man to realise she had crept out without her aunt's knowledge, and to get her inside without us being seen and anyone knowing she had ever been out of the house at all...

The worry was swept away with the sound of muffled thumps coming from inside the carriage. I veered over to the side of the country road and halted the horses, stepping down from my perch and opening the carriage door. What a sight I must have appeared, the man from the club and her all alone in a carriage, her friend nowhere in sight. She sat up, opened her eyes and mouth wide, and before she could scream I climbed inside and sat beside her, shushing her all the while.

Taking her hands in mine, I related what had happened and that Frances was safe at home. I asked how Pearl intended sneaking back inside herself, and she explained her plans in sleepy-voiced detail.

"It is not far to your house now, Pearl." I lifted one hand to brush away a stray hair from her cheek. "Dawn has arrived, so you may be seen by any servants you have. Can they be trusted?"

She nodded. "There is only one, Annabel, and she is late more often than not." Her body shook from either fright or the cold. Perhaps even both.

"Then we must hope she is late today. We must hurry. And," I stood in a crouch to exit the carriage, "I have not forgotten our dinner date tonight."

Pearl smiled wanly, her teeth chattering, and cloistered the blanket tighter around her. "Thank you. For this. For-"

"It has been my pleasure."

My God, I meant that. Despite the unsavoury turn of events, every minute spent in her company had been a pleasure. I left her seated and drove to her home, stopping the carriage on the road beside some trees marking the beginning of the driveway. I glanced at the house—no lights inside—and helped Pearl out, her cold, small hand dwarfed by mine.

"I will walk you to the house." I looked at it again, not wanting her to walk alone. That fellow could know her, know where she lived, and may well have been waiting to pounce from the trees at the back of the house. Wide columns flanked the front door, holding up a porch roof—a man could easily hide behind one of those. I know that was a terribly fanciful thing to think, but my need to protect this delicate gem of a woman had my mind envisaging many a scenario.

She did not protest, merely crooked her hand through my arm, and I smiled at the pleasure this gesture gave me. That she trusted me I had no doubt. Whether she would once she found out who I was remained to be seen. My plan was to have her enjoy my company, to want to see me time and again, and hopefully—dear God, how I hoped in that moment—my identity would not pose a problem by the time I had secured a place in her heart.

That also remained to be seen.

We walked up the drive, which curled to our right in front of the house and led to a side door that I presumed was the servants' entry. I waited until she had closed and locked the door behind her before I stole back down the driveway. A sense of loss encompassed me as I drove away, and I could not wait for tonight to come. As I journeyed, a

71

young woman, easily spotted as such by the light afforded from the now-rising sun, passed the carriage on a relatively new bicycle. I decided this was Pearl's maid and wondered whether her aunt had provided the means of transport, complete with a front basket that held a carpet bag. I could not imagine the maid being able to purchase the bicycle herself.

And so I arrived home, leaving the closing of the club to the appointed manager. Leaving the dreadful yet wonderful night behind. Such a mixture of emotions had gripped me, from lust to love to anger to hate, that I was quite spent by the time I climbed into bed. I stared around in the darkness, knowing every piece of furniture by heart, and wondered what Pearl's room was like. Did she have her bed positioned opposite the fireplace like I did? Did she own one bedside table or two? Perhaps she had a bookcase beside the fire, loaded with volumes that she read in a chair beside the window—just the same as me. I imagined Pearl tucked up in her bed, red hair spilling across the pillow, her hands clasped across her belly beneath the covers. Even the strain of my cock could not keep me awake, and I closed my eyes, hoping I slept well into the afternoon so that I did not have to wait long for the delights of the evening.

* * * *

I woke to the sound of birds chirping. The afternoon sun blared through my bedroom window. I had forgotten, in my tired state of a few hours previous, to close the curtains. Although I was weary of body, my mind was fully alert, and I sprang out of bed with the hope I would fool my weak limbs into thinking they had had enough rest. After a quick dip in the tub before the fire, the water brought by a servant lad who averted his gaze as he worked, my legs soon agreed that I was correct and proceeded to work in their usual fashion. I thanked the Lord for that.

While eating a hasty lunch alone at the large mahogany

dining table, that blasted room so long, so big and barren of a woman's touch, I pondered on how Pearl might change my home should I be lucky enough for her to live in it. Would she put colour on the walls, either with paint or paper? The whiteness of every wall in my home screamed of a man with no imagination, but that was far from the truth. I just did not have the time or inclination to have it decorated. Perhaps I could purchase some art so that when she visited here the place would not look so austere.

I made a late appearance at the brewery, apologising to Kenneth and giving him a vague explanation full of tosh that I had been unavoidably detained. I should not have even explained myself – he was paid to run the place after all – but my morals prompted me to, even if I did lie.

What a hypocrite I am. Am I pretending to be a man of good standing, when all along I am not? Surely that must be so if I am willing to feed my friend and manager untruths and keep the reality of who I am from Pearl. But...am I not doing the latter with good reason? If Pearl is able to see me for the man who loves her and not the one who she supposedly despises, will she not grow to love me too? I can only hope this is so.

Upon leaving the brewery, I stopped to purchase an evening paper, the headline leaving me chilled to the bone. The man who had been named Jack the Ripper had killed again. During the night! I devoured the words on the page, finding nothing much but the report of another woman being found slain in her bed. I would have to buy a paper on the morrow and hope more details were forthcoming. I had an uneasy feeling about that fellow who had accosted Pearl. My thoughts entertained the fact that he may have been the man the police sought, and although it was highly unlikely, just another of my fancies, there was a chance that he could be the one. And why not? He had certainly looked menacing enough and had used disgusting words when speaking to Pearl.

Either way, whoever he was, I intended to find him.

I gave my paper to a street urchin as I walked to the gentleman's club, intent on questioning the manager as to whether he, too, had seen that fellow last night. It was a long shot, a stab in the dark, but I would not be swayed.

I found John Robins polishing glasses in the empty bar, the doors not yet open to the public. He greeted me with a cheery grin and a nod of welcome, possibly assuming I would go straight to my office. His face clouded a little when I stood leaning on the bar, and he set a glass on to the shelf behind him, draping the towel over his shoulder.

"Everything all right, sir?"

His eyes held concern, and I wondered for a fleeting second whether he thought he had done something wrong. He rolled his burly shoulders, and not for the first time I congratulated myself on choosing him. There would be no trouble in this club, and if there was it would be quickly stopped with John Robins in charge. A strand of hair flopped over his brow, and he pushed it back, smiling somewhat uneasily through his close-cropped beard and moustache.

"Perfectly, except I wonder, did you happen to notice a fellow last night, talking to the new girl, Lily?" I prayed that he had—and knew who he was.

"That strange man? The one in the cloak and gloves?" John picked up another glass and began polishing.

I nodded.

"Oh, yes. I've seen him in the local pubs. Weird one. Stares at the women a bit too long for my liking. And not in a good way either."

"Ah, he is as I thought. Do you know him well?" I clenched my hands into fists, my heart beating fast as I hoped for the answer I sought.

"As it happens, I think he goes by the name of Percival Sloker. Bit of a mean fella by all accounts. I wouldn't want to meet him in a dark alley."

I remember thinking that I *would* want to meet him in a dark alley and this Percival Sloker would *not* wish to meet *me*. "Thank you, John." I paused, drumming my fingertips on the bar, then pushed myself off and strode to the main door. "I will not be in tonight. I have a dinner engagement. In fact, you may not see me until some time next week. If you have any problems in the meantime, send word via a lad."

John nodded. "Will do, sir. Have a good evening."

I realised as I made my way to the first public house along from the club that I had not asked what time I was expected at Pearl's. Pulling my pocket watch from beneath my outer coat, I glanced at its face. I supposed that eight o'clock would be a good time to arrive there and proceeded to enter a shabby public house that already had inebriated patrons propping up the bar. I had no idea whom to approach with regard to finding more information on one Percival Sloker, so I went to the bar with the intention of buying a small whisky to sip for the coming hour before I had to leave for Pearl's. It struck me as I swallowed the first burn of that amber liquid that I had not asked Pearl's aunt's permission to join them for dinner. I hoped the elderly woman would be grateful a suitor had come to dine and would allow me in without much preamble. I had heard she hated me too, and my heart sank. She might refuse my entry.

With my ponderings taking my attention, I had at first failed to look about the bar for the man I wanted to see. When I thought of Pearl, she dominated my thoughts, taking everything else from my mind. Not a good thing in this instance. As I looked up from studying the scarred wooden bar, I found him staring at me from directly across the room. My stomach lurched, and I straightened up. He eyed me with suspicion, then suddenly darted towards the door, fleeing outside.

I slammed my glass onto the bar and followed him, bursting out into the now-foggy night hoping that I would catch up with him. The tail of his cape flapped as he rounded the building down a side alley, and despite a tinge of fear inside me, I pursued. He waited halfway down, his body a shadow in the darkness, and without a thought as to what

I hoped to achieve, I ran towards him.

He lifted a hand in what I thought was a movement to strike, but as I drew closer he lowered it to his side. Something glinted in his grasp, and for the first time I doubted my sanity in this escapade.

"What do you want?" he asked, voice refined yet holding a hint of hoarseness.

"Just a question or two, if you please." I stood within feet of him, far enough away that if he held a knife he would have to lunge forward in order for it to pierce my body. "I have the unnerving thought that you are someone the authorities would be interested in. I have no basis for this other than the way you spoke to a certain young woman in my club during the night." My hands shook a little, anger, I supposed. I took a leap of faith and blurted what had been on my mind, stupid as it seemed. "And I saw news of another murder committed not a few hours ago. What of that?"

I sounded ridiculous, I knew that, but the words had poured out without my being able to stop them. They hung between us, heavy and mean, and I waited with my breath held for him to laugh and declare me insane.

"What of that?" he repeated, mocking me. His hand disappeared inside his cloak. "I may possibly be the one the law seeks, you are correct, but unless you tail me around these filthy streets every hour God sends, you will never know."

Was that a confession?

I bristled. "I have no intention of wasting my valuable time trailing you, sir. What I would ask, though, one gentleman to another, is that you refrain from visiting my club. I do not like the way you spoke to one of my staff."

"I shall speak to women however I like. You are not in a position to stop me." Silence dominated for a moment, then he said, "And if I wish to find that woman and speak to her in that manner again, showing her for the filthy harlot she is, I will do that also."

I shall not recount what happened next, only that I left that alley with a smile on my face and Percival Sloker knocked out, blood seeping from the back of his head as he lay sprawled on the cobbles, his knife down by his side.

I procured a cab to take me to Pearl's and write this account now by the light of a solitary gas lamp positioned above my head. The carriage trundles along her driveway, and I shall return this book to the inside flap of my coat and hope that her aunt will see sense and allow me to dine. The thought of what is to come churns my stomach, the excitement of spending time in Pearl's company and the trepidation of her aunt revealing who I am almost too much to bear.

As for Percival Sloker and what becomes of him, I can only hope that my warning does not go unheeded.

Chapter Six

November 9th, 1888

Pearl paced the drawing room rug, wringing her hands, her dark blue dress swishing around her ankles. She had not given the man a time and had realised, when her aunt had asked who was coming to dine, that she did not even know his name. How awful that she had not asked! How awful that it had not mattered.

Does not matter.

She lifted a hand to pat her hair, coiled on top of her head, and thought about earlier in the day. Her aunt had grumbled about the sudden request, lamenting that she felt unwell and did not need a night of entertaining. Pearl, ever the peacemaker, assured the old woman that she could dine alone with him, expecting a sharp retort and a refusal to her suggestion. It never came.

Her aunt had sighed. "Oh, what harm could it do just this once? It is not as though he would risk doing anything improper knowing I am in the house, and so long as he does not make it common knowledge that you dined alone..." The old woman had wandered from the drawing room, her mind seemingly elsewhere, a confused look on her face.

Pearl worried that her aunt was going senile but would contemplate that later. For now, time was on a mission and marched forward far too quickly for her liking. His imminent arrival was too close! Another thought struck her as she walked a track in the rug. What if he did not come at all? What if he had been toying with her at the club?

"No, he seemed sincere. A genuine man," she muttered,

dragging in a deep breath at the sound of wheels crunching the gravel outside.

She ran to the window and pulled aside the drapes, peering outside. A carriage approached, outer light swinging, and the sight of it brought Pearl's bottom to the window seat. Her pulse thudded dully, and she lifted a hand to her throat, watching the vehicle draw to a stop outside the house, the light hanging beside the front door offering scant illumination. The man had hired a hansom, the driver standing upright at the back, a long crop in hand and a top hat on his head. She stared inside the hansom, seeing only the club man's legs, his face obscured by the side of the cab, a black curtain across the window.

Giddy, Pearl stood and walked into the foyer, her shoes tapping the white marble tiles, legs unsteady and heart beating rapidly. She noted, as though for the first time, that the walls could do with repapering. The rose-pink paper had faded, the flowers on it blurry. She flushed with shame at what the man might think — that they were in need of funds or she was looking for a man to marry in order to take her away from this place.

Whatever had she done agreeing to this? Oh, she knew she did not have much of a choice — she needed his silence — but the way he made her feel spelled danger. She was not used to male company — not the kind where she was left breathless and out of sorts. The other men she had entertained in the past, for afternoon tea or the occasional dinner, had never caused her to lose her sense in this way.

Dear Lord, let me get through this evening without making a fool of myself.

She had instructed Annabel, the maid-cum-cook, to remain in the kitchen and only come out whenever Pearl rang the bell. Now, however, she re-examined her decision. Would it appear too improper that she answered the front door?

There was no time to debate the matter. A dark shape approached, and she watched it grow bigger through the glass in the door as he climbed the steps. With her mind awhirl, she blew out through pursed lips and swung the door wide, the smile on her face belying her inner turmoil.

By God he was a beautiful sight, one that would have swept her off her feet had she not prepared herself for just this event.

He tipped his hat. "Good evening, Pearl."

His voice melted her knees, and she pressed herself to the edge of the door in order to remain upright.

"Good evening...?" She tilted her head and raised her eyebrows.

He chuckled. "Ah. I never did give you my name. You may call me James. My middle name. I have never been partial to my first."

James. It did not suit him, but if that was what he wanted to be called then she would oblige him.

He cleared his throat. "I also did not ask to dine with you through the proper channels. The cab remains in case we have to postpone." He gestured behind him.

She studied his profile during the second he had looked away. She longed to reach out and touch his cheek, to run the backs of her fingers down the softness there. Blushing when he caught her looking, she stepped aside and allowed him entrance. "Oh, it is quite all right. My aunt is unwell and has — providing you promise to keep our dining a secret from those who enjoy scandal — given her permission that we dine alone. I assured her you were a man to be trusted." *Even though I have no idea whether you can be.*

He raised his eyebrows as he took off his hat and waved away the driver. "I have instructed the cab to return at ten. Is that too late?"

Pearl shook her head and closed the door, leaning back against it to give her knees time to regain their former rigidity. "No, not at all." *I wish you would stay longer.*

He took off his coat and instead of handing it to her, hung it on the hook beside the door. He stood so close that she smelt his pomade and the scent of outdoors. She wanted to press herself against him, and her wanton desires shook her to the core. How would she get through the evening without making some social *faux pas*, showing him he really should not be wasting his time with her? Surely he could see she was not the most experienced of hosts. She had not even taken his coat, for goodness sake!

"Oh. Please excuse me. I am not used to entertaining. And the maid... I asked Annabel to remain in the kitchen."

He raised his brows again. "Did you indeed?"

A sensual grin curved his lips, and if she had not known better she would have thought that there was something more than politeness in that smile. Or had she imagined it, wanting that to be so? As she had so many times in the past, she asked herself who wanted to marry a redhead? But she was a redhead only in colouring. She did not possess a bad temper, did not have a face full of freckles, and most certainly did not act like a spoilt brat. A man had said that to her once, when she had declined his offer of courting her. "A typical redhead, I see, one prone to acting like a spoilt child who stamps her feet..." Where he had got that idea she did not know.

Shoving those thoughts from her mind, she asked, "Would you care to go into the drawing room before dinner, or are you happy to eat straight away?"

"Dinner immediately will be fine, thank you. Please, lead the way."

She walked across the foyer and down a short hall beside the stairs opposite the front door, too conscious of him behind her. Was he studying her bottom, the sway of her hips? She chastised herself for thinking such a thing and turned into the dining room, stopping just inside the doorway so she could show James to his seat. Annabel had laid the table nicely, the place settings opposite one another at one end of the table. It stood in the centre of the room, matching sideboards either side of it against the walls. Vases and crystal bowls stood on top of them, ghosts of their shapes reflected on the highly polished wood. Heavy drapes at the windows at the far end kept the night at bay, and the room had an intimate feel to it. Pleased the maid had not let her down, Pearl strode inside and pulled out a chair.

"Ah, please allow me." James took over and gave a flourishing wave for Pearl to be seated. "I realise you are acting as host, but it would not be proper if I allowed you to let me sit before you."

"Thank you."

His thoughtfulness warmed her, and she sat, her face flushing as he stood behind her to push her chair forward. One of his hands brushed her shoulder—by design or accident she did not know—and she stifled a gasp at the jolt the touch gave her. The spot between her legs throbbed with sudden heat, and she laid her hands in her lap, feeling stupid for doing so because her secret desires were safe. She was not yet bold enough to flirt, nor was she about to tell him how he made her feel. It would not be right. They had met in a gentleman's club, of all places, and even though he had known she had not belonged there, it did not excuse the fact that she knew nothing whatsoever about him.

James sat and stared across the table at her, his gaze further flushing her cheeks. What on earth was it about this man that sent her into such a pathetic state? His magnetic presence, yes, that could be it, but for Pearl he presented a perfect package that would be hard to find elsewhere. She forced herself to speak. No one wanted a silent dinner companion.

"What were you—"

"How have you—"

He laughed at their dual outburst and lifted a carafe of water, filling their two glasses. "Please. You go first."

She cleared her throat. "What were you doing in that club?"

He smiled and gently placed the carafe down. "I could ask you the same question."

If her face grew any hotter, she would have to excuse

herself so she could splash it with cold water. "I... It was a stupid idea of Frances's. I should never have agreed. She wanted... We wanted to..." Could she tell him the truth? What would he think of her? And did it even matter? He had already seen her there and must know something afoot had been going on. "We wanted to see what it was like."

"Ah." He lifted his glass to smiling lips and sipped.

He swallowed, and she watched his Adam's apple bob. A shiver of that *something* ran down her spine.

"And you?" she asked. "What were you doing there?"

"I was there because I knew you would be."

His statement shocked her speechless for a moment. How had he known she would be there? Had Elizabeth told Gerald their plans, and had he, in turn, told this man?

"Oh." She could manage no more so rang the bell in the centre of the table.

"Does that surprise you?" James lowered his glass to the table and circled the rim with one finger.

"It does. I do not understand why you would wish to be there because of me." *Unless Elizabeth had sent him to spy! The little –*

"I have wanted to be near you for a long time, Pearl. I have not had the courage to come calling because – "

Annabel breezed in, pushing a serving trolley laden with silver-domed bowls and a gravy jug. The conversation ceased while she busied herself placing the bowls on the table, and Pearl lowered her gaze until Annabel was done.

"We can serve ourselves, thank you, Annabel." Pearl lifted her head to smile at her. "I will ring again when we have finished."

The maid bobbed and wheeled the trolley to stand it beside the door before she left the room.

"Would you like me to serve?" Pearl asked, lifting the lids. "Ah, I see Annabel has made everything I asked."

James reached across, stilling her arm as she moved to place a lid on the table. "I will serve."

Her hand shook. She stared at him, wanting to thank him

for his gentlemanly behaviour but failed to find the words. If she was rendered mute by his fingers curling around her wrist, what would she be like if he touched her?

"I…" *How will I get through the next hour or so?*

Pearl got through it with a struggle to keep her hands to herself. She was surprised by the urges she experienced during the meal. At one point, James had a speck of gravy on his lip that she longed to lick away. Such thoughts were not proper for a woman of her standing, yet she thought them all the same. Perhaps she was not normal. Perhaps she had been born into the wrong class, for she had been led to believe that women of her class endured the attentions of their husbands with only the desire to create new life in mind.

She did not want to create new life in that sense. No, she wanted to create a life for herself with James in it, his hands upon her body and his mouth upon hers. Now, she bit her lower lip as they stood in the foyer waiting for his hansom to arrive. It was late, but Pearl did not mind. She did not want the hansom to arrive at all.

"I have had a lovely evening, Pearl. Thank you." James shrugged on his coat. "Would I be allowed to call again? Perhaps during the day? We could stroll around the grounds. Or maybe your aunt would like to join us on a ride into the city?"

My aunt. Does she have to come?

She ignored his suggestion, not wishing to entertain sharing this man with anyone. "Is my seeing you again a sign that I have not fulfilled my end of the bargain? That I must see you once more to keep my being at the club a secret?" Surely he only wanted to see her for that reason.

But his actions over dinner proved otherwise. He was polite, attentive and he looked at me with what I hope was fondness, or perhaps something close to that. A liking of me.

She studied him as he weighed his answer, the silence between them a tangible thing that was not uncomfortable but quite the opposite.

I want to see him every day. Alone. I want him to touch me in places only I have touched. I want —

"If you will permit it, I would like to court you." His dark eyes grew hooded, the look he gave her sensual, setting her heart to racing.

"You would? Oh." She lowered her head, unable to look at him any longer. She did not trust herself to remain the kind of woman he should be courting.

He lifted his hand and settled the side of one finger beneath her chin, raising her face so she looked up at him. Stepping closer, their chests inches apart, he trailed his thumb over her lips. Desire ricocheted through her, spreading to her fingertips and the ends of her toes. She blushed yet again, staring into eyes that were so deep she could get lost in them. Boldly, she dashed out her tongue, immediately appalled by her behaviour.

"I am so sorry. I—"

James dipped his head and brushed his lips against hers, and oh my, Pearl's toes curled and the throb between her legs began again. She clenched her legs together, breaths coming hard and fast, and he kept his lip brushes non-intrusive, a feather-light joining that drew a whimper from her. She came to her senses at a creak from above and sprang away from him on wobbly legs.

Hand to her chest, face burning, she said, "Oh! What you must think of me. I am so terribly sorry."

Spots of red coloured his cheeks, and he panted. "No, it is I who should apologise. I have treated you badly. Please forgive me. I could not help myself."

He could not help himself. Oh my God.

Flustered, she straightened her dress even though it did not need straightening and patted her hair even though not one tress was out of place. They stared at one another, and she wanted nothing more than to fling herself at him like the wanton woman she was inside and have him take her there and then. Carnal images flickered through her mind, causing her cheeks to heat some more, and oh, the beat between her legs to increase.

The sound of the hansom driving over the gravel filtered through the front door, erasing the scenes only she saw. Swinging open the door so nothing else untoward could occur, Pearl smiled brightly and welcomed the cool air to her face.

James laid a hand on her arm. "Please, am I forgiven?"

She nodded. "Yes, of course."

"And will we meet again?"

Yes. I wish you did not have to go. I wish – "Yes. We will."

The hansom pulled to a stop outside, and Pearl glanced at the driver. He faced forward, head slightly bent, but although she had the urge to press a quick kiss on James's cheek she did not dare. She wanted to take the look of sorrow from his face and let him know she was as much to blame for what had happened as he was.

"It is quite all right," she whispered, looking into his eyes. "I loved it."

Quickly, she pushed him out the door and closed it tight, rushing into the drawing room so she could peer through the window. She sat on the sill seat and inched the drapes apart where they met in the middle. James still stood on the top step, staring at the front door with one hand raised, as though he intended to knock. He dropped it to his side then, swirling to face the hansom and walking towards it with a slow pace. He did not want to leave, and Pearl could not believe it. He liked her!

As he climbed aboard and settled into his seat, Pearl acted on impulse and flung the drapes wide. Excited by her disregard for what was proper, she hefted up the window and stuck her head out.

"When will you call again?" she asked, pleased that James snapped his head up to look at her, a wide smile on his face. "So you can do that some more."

He widened his eyes, and a quiet but hearty laugh filled the air. "Soon, Pearl. Very soon."

The driver cracked his whip, and the carriage jerked into

motion. James raised a hand in farewell before the cab turned and headed towards the road. A sinking feeling pulled at Pearl's belly, and although breathless at her behaviour, she felt deflation creeping upon her. Once the cab was out of sight, she pulled the window down, securing the lock then closing the drapes. As she began to turn from the window, a shadow in the doorway caught her eye and she gasped, facing it fully to take in who stood there.

"I'll be off home now, miss," Annabel said, a cheeky smile on her lips.

Oh, God. She heard what I said!

Clearing her throat and trying to ignore the burn of her cheeks, Pearl said, "I think it is rather late for you to be out on your bicycle. Especially with that dreadful murderer on the loose. I feel it would be better that you stayed here for the night."

"As you say, miss." Annabel curtseyed and left the room.

Pearl watched her through the doorway, the young woman climbing the stairs quietly, and she wondered if Annabel had sampled the delights of a kiss as beautiful as the one she herself had been given.

Mind full of James, Pearl doused the lights and retired to her room. She lit a candle on the sideboard beside the door then disrobed, washing at the bowl there. The cold water shocked her into being fully alert, and she dried off then slipped on a nightgown. She turned, looking at her room, trying to imagine how it would appear to someone else. To a man. To James.

It was basic, the small touches from her youth gone now—a teddy bear who used to sit on her bed, a doll that had rested in its carriage, the childish books that had sat in a pile on the windowsill. Her bed, one that used to have white drapes she could close once she had climbed in, was now just a place to sleep, the pink comforter no comfort at all. She looked around again, wondering if this was what she would forever have—a room without a man to share it with. A small vanity beside her sideboard where she would sit and gaze at her ageing reflection as the lonely years passed her by. She sighed, then eased between the chilly sheets to wait for sleep to come.

It did not. Pearl lay there for what seemed an eternity, the shadowed ceiling offering nothing to relieve her restlessness. Perhaps hours had passed, or maybe long minutes that stretched out and fooled her into thinking more time had gone by, but a sharp sound like scattering gravel rent the air, halting time completely. She sat upright, the sheet clutched to her breast, and listened for the sound again. For any noise that told her she had not imagined the first. There it was again, a shower of gravel as though it had been thrown and now slapped back to the ground. Was Annabel up and about out there?

Frowning, Pearl got out of bed and padded to the window, the chill in the air springing goose-bumps on her skin. She shifted one heavy velvet drape across and stared down at the driveway. James stood just in front of the steps, his face appearing to sit on the stone overhang above the front door. What the devil was he doing out there? Had something happened that she should know about? Something to do with Frances? Alarmed, Pearl unlocked the window and eased it upward, leaning her hands on the sill and poking her torso out. James looked up, appearing somewhat abashed.

"What has happened?" she called in an urgent whisper. "Is it Frances?"

"Uh, no." James stepped back so she could see all of him, bent his head and stared at the ground, finger and thumb toying with his chin. "I…" He stared up again. "I could not stand going home. I wanted…to come back. Be with you. Stupid of me, I know, because we can't possibly —"

"Wait there." Pearl lowered the window, her whole body tingling. She felt so alive she wanted to cry and laugh at the same time. What on earth had possessed him to risk coming back? Her aunt…Annabel… "Stuff them!" she declared quietly, taking her robe from the hook on the back of the door and draping it around her shoulders.

She lit out of her room and ran quietly along a short hallway, grasping the newel post and swinging herself around, taking the stairs at a quick pace. She slid her arms into her gown, belted it, and headed towards the front door. His shadowy form stood behind the glass, close to the door. Her heart pattered violently, and her pulse thrummed in her ears. Stomach rolling, she drew back the bolts quietly and opened the door, slipping outside.

"I cannot believe you are here, James! Whatever would happen if we were caught?" She longed to touch his hair, bury her hand in it and draw his face to hers for a kiss.

"The same as if you were caught at my club." He widened his eyes, realising his slip of the tongue.

Far from revolting her, the idea of him owning that place intrigued her. It was so…naughty for a man of his standing. "*Your* club?"

"Yes, but it is not like you may think. I wanted somewhere safe for those women to work. I do not plan to go there as a rule. I have a manager. I—"

She stood on tiptoes and rested a finger over his lips. He smelt divine, of outdoors and a spicy pomade. The contact and aroma sent desire straight to her core. "You do not need to explain. Will we take a walk?" She stared into his eyes, mesmerised by them.

"It is a little cold, and you do not have anything on your feet. I would not like you to catch a chill. I just wanted to see you again. I should go." He stepped back one pace, his hand brushing down her arm.

That touch and the memories of that man touching the madam spurred her to say, "My bedroom then?" She quirked an eyebrow in question but also surprise at her thoughts having tumbled from her lips. He *would* think her loose. Wanton. A woman free with her favours.

Did she care? On the one hand she did, but on the other… no, she did not. If she was destined to spend the rest of her life alone, she would take this night and all it had to offer,

society be damned.

Chapter Seven

The Diary of Seth Adams

November 10th, 1888

I stared at her when she said "My bedroom then?" and wondered if I had misheard. Surely she had not uttered the words I had wanted to hear for such a long time. For a moment society did not matter but what she had said did. My morals reared up, large and looming, smacking me back to reality with an ungodly thump.

"That would not be proper," I said, hating those words as they left my lips.

She appeared ashamed, her cheeks flushing and her eyes half closing, as though I thought she was a harlot for her suggestion. Another man might have done, but I did not. After all, those were the words I have longed to hear since I saw her for the first time. She captured me with not only her beauty but also a grace that seemed to shine from her, even though she was clearly devastated by her parents' deaths. I stood at the back of the mourning crowd the day they were buried and watched her, a broken bird, unable to fly among the guests, her wings too heavy to lift.

Yet outside her front door she appeared as a phoenix, rising from the ashes, and I could not help but wonder how she would look at me once my identity became clear. And it would, of that I was certain. The sight would crush me.

She placed a hand on my wrist, her skin so delicate the veins showed beneath, and my heart stilled for two beats. I could not breathe, such was the energy that transferred from her to me.

"Please. I liked it last time. I want to try it again. The kiss."

Oh, such innocence, such pure naivety. She had no inkling of what trying it again could lead to, I was sure. Could I do as she asked? It was quite improper, and if I were any kind of gentleman I would have refused once again and walked away. Were I any kind of gentleman, I would not have come back at all after we had dined. I should have stayed away and called in the daytime, asking her aunt's permission to court her niece.

Yet I had not, and there I stood, dallying on which option to take.

Then she said, "Please, I will not tell. No one will know." She smiled and lowered her eyelids but looked up at me through auburn lashes. "Besides, I did not get to continue my experience at the club. I do not fully know what those women do. I wish for you to show me."

What she had asked of me was too much, for I could not sully her as I would a woman who was free with her favours for a living. But...damn, I allowed her to draw me inside her home and up the stairs to a room with a double bed. The covers were rumpled from where she had been beneath them prior to my return, the bottom sheet bearing the imprint of her body, the pillow dented from her head. Apart from a sideboard beside the door, her room was nothing like I had imagined. No bookcases. No chair by the window. I hoped that when she—if she—were to become my wife, she would feel free to express herself by redecorating my home. It appeared her room was as sparse as my life before she had entered it.

She locked the door and moved towards the bed, and my mind was awhirl with being caught and the scandal it would cause. It would not faze me in the slightest, for I would marry her in a heartbeat, but I had to think of her reputation.

"Pearl, we must stop this now before we go too far. It is not right that I am here. I should not have come back." I stepped towards her, arm outstretched and curled my fingers around her wrist. That energy again hit me hard and my cock responded to our being together, close, and in a bedroom.

"Does it feel wrong in here?" she asked, raising one hand to her chest. "It does not for me. It feels…the most correct thing to do." She glanced back at the bed, the vein pulsating in her neck.

I wanted to kiss it, to run my tongue up that slender column to her ear and suck the lobe into my mouth.

She turned back to face me. "I realise I do not know you, and I also realise how ludicrous this is, how…others would see it. But there is something about you." She cocked her head, studying me, and I found that I enjoyed her scrutiny. "That I cannot deny."

For a woman who had never been bedded, she seemed to know exactly what she wanted, and the fleeting thought that she *had* done this before swept through my mind. But no, I had heard through my extensive yet secretive queries about her that she was quite the innocent. What was making her behave this way? Could it be true that she felt something for me, recognised what I had – that some spark, some *thing* existed between us, even though we were relative strangers?

"Pearl… I would not be any kind of good man were I to take you up on your offer. I am not any kind of good man to be standing here now. I –"

She stilled my words with a finger to my lips, and by God I resisted the urge to dash out my tongue and lick the tip. To suck that digit into my mouth and watch her blush.

"Hush," she said. "I invited you inside. I want another… kiss. And more."

"What has made you ask such a thing?" I had to know whether my enquiries about her had been thorough enough. She appeared innocent yet at the same time versed in what she wanted.

"I…" She blushed. "At the club, I saw something I should

93

perhaps not have seen."

What on earth could she mean? "What did you see?"

"I was invited to watch…something." She looked down.

I lifted her chin with a finger. "Watch what?"

"The madam and a man."

Christ, when did that happen? Where the devil was I? What had taken my attention over knowing where she was at all times?

"How did it make you feel?" I was curious to know. My musings when with Charlotte about whether Pearl would be a willing and enthusiastic bed partner came to mind.

"I felt ashamed, but only after…after…"

"After what?" I stared into her eyes.

"After I had gained pleasure from watching. I want to try those things. I want you to do to me what he did to her." She wrenched her chin from my grasp and stared to the side. "I am wretched," she whispered.

"No! No, you are not. It is a natural reaction. It was not your fault."

That madam had a lot to answer for.

"So it is not wrong of me to want you to kiss me? Please. I want that kiss."

And I was undone. Her final word had trailed to a whisper, seductive and enthralling, and I gripped her wrist and lowered her hand from my lips. Tilting my head, I took her mouth in a hungry kiss, spearing my tongue between her soft lips and probing inside. Perhaps I should have been gentler, but the fire raging inside me and my cock swelling took away all reason. She asked and I gave, and her moan of pleasure as my tongue explored further ignited my desire. It was wrong, my mind continued to scream that, but as she had said, it did not feel wrong in my heart.

She lifted her arms, buried her fingers in my hair, and I drew her closer, my hands about her back. Heat from her body warmed my skin, and the need to show her how fiercely I loved her fought with my yen to treat her with a tender hand. I was caught in a firestorm, one that refused to let me go.

Pearl pressed her breasts to my chest. The feel of those swells made my cock grow harder, and God, I wanted to take her, to push inside her, cover her body with mine. She had not asked for that so I did not press for it, but instead kissed her fervently and with much pleasure.

She broke away first, laying her hands on my shoulders and staring up at me with kiss-swollen lips and a flush to her cheeks. She looked utterly desirable, this beauty of mine, who stood breathless in my arms. My cock throbbed painfully — it had been some time since I had engaged in contact with a woman this way — but the throb was greater than any I had felt before. She had cast some trickery upon me, where I was powerless to refuse anything she wished.

"Show me," she said, eyes beseeching, fingertips digging into my flesh. "Show me how it feels to be kissed down... *there*."

The shock of her request almost sent me reeling backward, but I remained in place, head lightening, my knees weak. How was it that such a woman unversed in sexual experiences could render me so feeble? I was pliant in her arms, a man ready to do her bidding. My mind continued to scream of how wrong this was, but the moment had captured me in its grasp. Her voice, with its innocent lilt, and her request, given as though nothing more than a trivial one, left me stunned. How could I deny her?

I could not.

She went to the bed, climbing on to the mattress, her gaze fixed on my face. And I stood unable to refuse, my heart beating too fast, my hands itching to glide beneath her nightgown and caress every inch of her, every rise and dip. She positioned herself in the centre of the bed, hands flat to the mattress behind her, weight braced upon them. With what I sensed was deliberate slowness and a move born of listening to her heart rather than from experience, she eased her legs up so her nightgown slid down her thighs and to the juncture at the top of them.

Ah, I watched her intently then, feasting on the sight

before me. Slender calves tapered to pretty little ankles, pressed together to deny my sight of what rested between her legs. My breath caught, and she regarded me with a twinkle in her eye that had not been present seconds before. She pushed out her chest, and her breasts jutted beneath the fabric, her hard nipples perking, goading me to rub a thumb across them and feel their rigidity. I held back from joining her on the bed, not wishing to do anything she did not request. Standing there would have been enough had she told me to leave—or so I told myself—but a longing overtook me, almost strange in its intensity, and I knew it would have pained me to walk away.

Her cheeks flushed, the rosy hue quite becoming, and she pouted, sweeping her gaze low then lifting her head to stare directly at me. Like a challenge had been issued, she continued to look at me as I did the same to her, forcing myself not to move unless invited. And then slowly she parted her knees, revealing the beauty resting there, that dark russet hair and the slit I had coveted for so long. The scent of her arousal reached me, heady, a tang unlike any other, and I wanted to kneel before her and bury my face in her folds.

Knees against the mattress, the soles of her feet pressed together, Pearl dared me with her eyes to take a sup. I looked from her face to her cleft then back again, the fight against following what my heart desired a struggle I would not be able to contend with for much longer.

Speak, my love. Tell me what you want.

"I often wondered," she said, "what a woman of the night would call...this." She looked down at her thatch. "I know now and can use that word myself."

She took my breath away with her daring, her innocence so prominent despite what she had said. I adored her in that moment. Utterly adored her.

"I feel badly that you were exposed to such a word in my establishment," I managed. "You should not have been invited upstairs."

"It does not matter." She raised her head to stare at me again. "You would deny me the whole experience?"

Good Lord, she addled my senses, left them spinning in all directions with every word she uttered.

"I would deny you nothing, but—"

"Then you will allow me to say it?"

The scent of her grew stronger, seemingly swirling around me like perfume. "I will, although I wish to state I am not wholly comfortable with it."

"Tonight I am not a lady, you know that. So please…let me say it. If it makes you feel better, you say it first."

"Cunt," I whispered, the word too damn rude and too damn erotic.

"Louder. Say it louder."

"Cunt."

My bollocks throbbed, ached with such ferocity I thought I would ejaculate. I longed to free my cock and fist it, bringing myself to completion as I had in the club, but her very presence held me still and unwilling to undo the buttons that would give my hardness liberty.

"Cunt," she said, trying the word for herself. "Well then, James, I want you to lick my cunt."

I gasped. "What on earth made you say that?"

She blushed. "The madam. She used that word. It sounded so…good. I wanted to try it for myself. To act like her."

She lifted one hand from the bed and beckoned me forward. Her chest rose and fell rapidly, the breaths huffing from between her half-parted lips a symphony to my ears. I took one step forward and faltered. What she had asked would take us into new territory. What if she regretted it on the morrow? What if she refused to see me again?

I could not bear that.

"Are you certain this is what you want?" I asked, trying to control myself—it was so damn difficult to remain where I was.

"Yes. Come here."

I stood close to the bed, and she moved her feet apart,

97

pressing the soles to the mattress. My excitement was reaching a dangerous level. If I was not careful, controlled... I kneeled on the bed and settled between her legs, keeping eye contact with Pearl. I wanted the whole of her, heart, body and soul, and I would not rest until I had it.

She stared at me, those big, innocent eyes of hers doing things to my insides that told me I was well and truly lost to her. I would do anything—I knew in that moment she could have requested the moon and I would have done everything in my power to fetch it for her. I wanted to touch, to reach out and run my hands over the fabric hiding her upper body from my sight, but I held back. Pearl would have to ask.

"Come now, James. You would not want to keep me waiting, would you?"

Pearl tilted her head and gave a smile that warmed more than my heart. My cock was on fire, and I clenched my fingers to stop myself lifting her nightgown farther and seeking out the delights beneath. I imagined her breasts, how the curved plumpness would feel in my palm, and a fierce ache intensified in my bollocks to such a degree that I held my breath.

Caught between obeying her and knowing what I was about to do was wrong, I hesitated before bowing my head to her silky folds. The scent of her goaded me to sup, to savour the taste of it on my tongue, and a blush crept into my face, embarrassment that if she could read my thoughts...

"Please. My cunt is aching."

Her words widened my eyes and had my heartbeat stuttering. By God, she was a treasure. A beautiful, adorable treasure. Her lips bent into a coy smile, the Cupid's bow pronounced and begging mine to press against them.

My thoughts raced. *This is wrong yet it is not. I should not do as she asks for obvious reasons, yet I know I cannot deny her. But also...I have hidden who I am from her. There is an issue of trust. How has she never set eyes upon me, the man she claims to hate? Has she secluded herself away to the point she does not see anyone – anyone at all apart from her friends? Why, then, would she even entertain me here this night? Surely her yearning to see how the other half live should not extend to something so... intimate. So drastic.*

She moaned, a pained sound that pulled me from my reverie. She puffed out her cheeks, the rosy hue growing deeper, and blew out a steady breath through those perfect lips of hers. What would happen after this night? Would she allow me to return, or was I just an experiment? Did it matter?

God, yes, it matters. I want her to want me. Always.

I did not ask the many questions roaming through my mind, but pressed my hands to the mattress either side of her waist, dipped my chin and stared at her cunt. I had not been with a woman since my last time with Charlotte, and I yearned for the comfort and closeness being with Pearl would bring.

She glistened with cream, a cream that smelt of promise, and I licked my lips. I felt her studying me, heard the anticipation in her uneven breaths, the slight catch of air in her throat as I lowered my head a little more. Her heart must have been beating wildly, for she was a woman as yet untouched by any man. I have had my share of women, know how they feel and taste, but my heart drummed a cadence it had never drummed before.

I glanced up at her face, her lashes almost gracing the swell of her cheeks. Her lips were parted just a touch. Her eyes shone with excitement and, if I detected correctly, a hint of fear. Perhaps she thought then of the consequences should she be found out, and I admired her for trusting me in keeping my mouth sealed once I left her home. After all, she did not know me, had nothing but her instincts to follow with regard to my honour.

Once again I felt compelled to ask, "Are you sure?"

She hitched in a breath and nodded, catching her full bottom lip between her teeth. I stared at her for what seemed an eternity, waiting for her to change her mind. My God, I did not want her to. When she raised her hips and gave a soft gasp, I slid my hands beneath her buttocks and took my first taste of her.

Gliding my tongue from her opening to her bud was, indeed, a taste of promise, of more to come. She gasped, a sharp sound that sent me drowning, and buried one hand in my hair. The sensuous exploration of her fingertips on my scalp goaded a moan from me...how I had longed for this to happen. Her flavour coated my tongue, and her scent filled my nose. Combined with the softness of her buttocks in my hands, the sensations I experienced were like no others. Tingles spread through me, originating in my cock, and the twinge in my bollocks bordered on pain. I drew my tongue down then up again, swirling the tip around her bud, and her buttocks tautened with another lift of her hips. That she pushed herself against my tongue excited me beyond measure, and while still teasing her folds, I took a moment to coach myself into giving her pleasure and not indulging in my own.

It proved difficult. Just being with Pearl tested my ability to remain strong. Cock dripping with my own cream, I licked her softness with light strokes, knowing by instinct that she needed for me to be gentle.

Her barely perceptible "Ah!" quickened my heartbeat, then she murmured, "Oh, James, I love you licking my cunt."

She knew how to ratchet up a man's desire, innocent or not. She was a natural. Her words made me want to free my cock and thrust inside her, making her fully mine. I wanted to press my naked body to hers, hold her close and ease in and out of her slick channel, our skin wet with sweat.

Dear God, let that happen soon.

I laved her harder, flicking my tongue back and forth across her engorged nub. She writhed and fisted my hair, delicate pants issuing from her pretty mouth. I looked up to see her reaction as I applied more pressure, moved my tongue faster. The devil must have instructed her, for, unlike any woman I had shared a bed with before, she watched me. She slid her tongue across her lips, mimicking the movement of mine, only with slower, more languid strokes. The sight almost pushed me over the edge.

And then she could take no more. A long, drawn-out groan burst out of her, and she widened her eyes a second before her hips jolted. I continued to watch her reaction, continued to sup her cream and tend to her bud. She fell backward, gripping the covers with her free hand and tightening her fist in my hair. Hips raising, she balanced herself on just her feet and shoulders, her knees clamped to the sides of my arms. I held her in place and sped the pace of my tongue, intent on witnessing her facial expression as her first sexual release from a man stormed through her.

Pearl's mouth formed an O, and at last she closed her eyes. She groaned, soft lilts of sound that had my heart and cock singing, and thrashed her head from side to side. Her abdomen bucked, and I held her tighter, worked my tongue faster, kneading the flesh of her bottom. She rode out her release well, and as I sensed her coming back down from the peak, I relented on the pressure and licked her softly, allowing her time to adjust to her body returning to normal.

I lowered her, giving one last swipe of my tongue, and she released my hair, her hand flopping to the bed. Smoothing my palms over her belly, I straightened and waited for her to open her eyes. Her chest rose and fell rapidly, and her breaths were hard and raspy. She smiled then opened her eyes, staring directly at me.

"James, that was…wonderful. I…I had no idea it could be so…" She lifted her hands then let them drop back to the bed. "Is there a way I can do the same for you?" She eased up on to her elbows.

I swallowed, unsure whether I had heard her correctly. In my experience, women—good, decent women—did not do such things. "I… There is, but it is not something you should be thinking about. A woman of your—"

101

"Then tell me what I must do. Tonight, I am not myself, remember?"

She eyed me with such a coy yet intense stare I found it impossible to look away. She had enchanted me, cast a spell that I knew would never be broken. I would follow her to the ends of the earth if that was her wish, but what she was implying…

"Pearl, I…it does not feel right that you should do *that*."

But I want you to. My God, I want your sweet lips around me.

She sat upright, head tilted, a frown drawing her brows towards the top of her nose. "It does not feel right? Do you not want me to do that?"

Her position before me, legs still splayed, her cunt open for my inspection, her scent, all drove me mad with desire. "Yes, I want you to do that, but—"

"Then if you want it, I shall do it."

Pearl drew her legs back and settled on her knees. Inches from me, she raised a hand and touched my cheek. I closed my eyes, for her touch felt like Heaven. She pressed her lips to mine. She slid her tongue into my mouth, a daring, bold move for a woman such as she, and I could not resist joining her in the kiss. Could she taste herself?

I gave in to my needs and embraced her, crushing her body to mine and sinking my fingers into her hair. A whimper sounded in her throat, and the heat of her hand as she placed it on my lower back set my cock to throbbing harder.

This woman, this beautiful creation, had my mind awhirl with possibilities and hopes for the future. I could not let her go now that I had sampled her delights. I wanted to marry her, teach her the wonders of sex and bring her to new heights every time.

I could not—would not—let her go.

She ended the kiss, and I opened my eyes to find hers closed, a small smile playing about her lips. It was as though she had to take a moment to consider what had happened, to savour it before moving on to… Could I stand her sucking my cock? Could I allow her to do such a thing? The thought of it alone made me want to spill my seed.

Pearl opened her eyes and cradled my face with both hands. "So tell me...what I have to do. Teach me to suck your cock."

Chapter Eight

November 10th, 1888

Something had taken over Pearl, a longing to experience, to give, to be in control. Too often lately she had felt things were out of her control, her life directed by rules set by both society and her aunt. She must behave this way, smile at appropriate moments, sit in the blasted drawing room sewing stitch after stitch on handkerchief after handkerchief, the ends of her thumb and finger sore...

Not this night. No, she wanted to have something for herself, something *she* governed, and sucking James's cock was the perfect opportunity to experience the heady thrill she had had at the club. How different it had been there. Oh yes, she had been afraid, that someone she knew would walk in or that horrible man would overstep the invisible line of civility and force her to do something she would most certainly not want to do, but the freedom...she had never felt so alive.

And the show she'd witnessed, the madam and the man... God help her, but she had thought of it many times since. Had closed her eyes and remembered every detail, wanting to fondle herself to completion. And now she understood why the madam had keened when the man licked her. She had wanted to scream out the same way but had held back through fear of her aunt hearing her. But oh, how she had longed to show James with sound how much she loved what he had done, how knowing what it felt like far surpassed watching it being done.

James's face...he appeared both shocked and pleasantly

surprised by her words, yet must have had an inkling of what she had in mind before she had said that deliciously rude word. Cock. Perhaps he had previously seen her as a staid female who had never even heard of the word. She enjoyed shocking him, and despite that, a small part of her worried that once this was over, once she had allowed him to have all of her, he would leave, never to return.

But I will not think of that now. Not yet.

She lowered her gaze to his groin and listened to the sweet sound of his breathing. It had quickened. Pleased she affected him so, she took a moment to study how his erection pushed against the fabric hiding him from view. What would he look like? Prior to seeing the man at the club, she had never seen a penis, had only imagined one from the descriptions Elizabeth had given after her wedding night. Would he be long and thin, or short and wide? Would it hurt when he pushed inside her, like Elizabeth had said? Pearl had no doubt it would, but her cunt ached with the need to have him fill her, for her to surrender herself to him in ways a lady should not want. Should not need.

But tonight I am not a lady.

"Pearl, I—"

"Shh."

Without looking up at him, she grasped his wrists, moving his hands to settle on her shoulders. The heat from the contact soared through her, sending a thrill to her core. How could a man affect her this way? Why had Elizabeth pronounced intimacy as awkward and messy? It had not been so far for Pearl and was not now. It was delicious, touching, hot and exciting.

She trailed her fingertips over his hardness, surprised at the heat there. With her stomach in knots—Lord, the excitement was too much—she lifted her gaze to stare into his eyes as she freed him. The soft skin brushed her thumb for a second and the swift contact set her bud to throbbing. Her head lightened—so much to take in at once!—and she pulled in a lungful of air to steady her breathing. James stared at her as though teetering on telling her he could not allow her to continue, so she wrenched her gaze from his mesmerising eyes and looked down.

Oh my. His shaft jutted outward, long *and* wide, the skin an altogether different colour from that on his body. It was a shade darker, and a bulging vein snaked up his length. It did not repulse her as Elizabeth had led her to believe it would, but rather piqued her curiosity, and she lowered her head for a better look. His tip, bulbous and a beautiful shade of light lilac, fascinated her with its glistening moisture. Was this the "repulsive" liquid Elizabeth had mentioned? It did not look repulsive. It looked enticing, and Pearl dipped her head farther. She breathed in, and a new scent filled her nose, one for which she had no name. Tilting her head, she reached out and took him in hand. Oh, how the warmth of him heated her palm, how it fitted there as though made just for her. She stared in wonder at his seeping tip peeking out of her grip and marvelled at how his shaft twitched and pulsed. Had she made it do that?

James groaned and took one hand from her shoulder to bury it in her hair. "Pearl, tell me how you feel."

She hesitated to reply in order to think. How *did* she feel? "Excited, frightened, awed, giddy… I want…I want to lick your wetness away."

"Oh, God. You have no idea how much pain I am in."

"Pain?" She glanced up sharply, frowning, and let go of him. "Am I hurting you?"

"No. No! The pain is not *that* kind. It is a sweet pain where you are torturing me with your touch. I want more but I am afraid to push you too quickly."

"I do not know what I have to do. You are supposed to teach me." She breathed in and out slowly, getting a dose of that wonderful smell with no name. "Tell me what I have to do."

James moaned, the sound deep and guttural. "Move your hand up and down. Softly. Slowly."

Pearl looked down at her hand. Despite his hardness,

she worried she might hurt him. Tentatively, she did as he asked, and his loud groan startled her into letting him go again.

"No, please. Do it again."

She glanced up to make sure he meant it, and by the look on his face — a soft smile, twinkling eyes, and a quick nod — she returned her gaze to his shaft. And her hand to his cock. Taking a deep breath, she massaged his length, loving how he felt so delicate yet rigid at the same time. His breathing quickened some more and hers matched it. The bead of liquid dripped down his rounded tip and pooled on the web of skin between her thumb and finger. Its wetness made her stomach clench — this was so exhilarating, so naughty — and without giving herself time to ponder her instincts, she bent to lick the fluid away. Her tongue brushed his cock, and the taste of him spread on her tongue, salty but not unpleasant. And she wanted more.

"Hold me at the base and lick me."

His words... God, how they sent her mind whirling. She moved her hand down, his dark nest of hair tickling her skin, and positioned herself comfortably. His fingers played with her curls and teased her scalp, his other hand on her shoulder. She flicked out her tongue, his softness a surprise. She had expected hardness. Yes, he was that, but the mix of hard and soft was something she had yet to understand.

"Flatten your tongue and lick from bottom to top."

His fingers tightened a little on her shoulder, then relaxed. Pearl pressed her tongue against him and dragged it up his length, tasting more of his fluid as she finished the stroke.

"Again. Do it again."

Pearl complied, growing bolder with every lick, swirling her tongue around the head each time she reached the top. She took James's moans as those of pleasure, that she was doing this correctly, so she laved him more fluidly.

"Now put your lips around me. Take me into your mouth."

As she glided her tongue upward, her breaths coming

fast and ragged, she closed her lips over his tip. Could she really do this? Take him in her mouth? His tip was wide, and her teeth settled against him. She wondered if she would be able to accommodate this new intrusion with ease. She relaxed her jaw.

"Now take me deeper."

Pearl removed her hand and flattened her palm over his wiry hairs.

I can do this. I am Lily, a woman of the night.

She drew him inside her mouth, lips stretching, tongue curling around him. His tip butted the back of her throat, and she eased back, fighting the urge to gag.

"Careful. Not too deep. Not just yet. Not until you are more used to it." He sucked in a breath and released it slowly. "My God, Pearl, I am trying so hard not to…"

She took him deeper again, too engrossed in what she was doing to ponder overmuch on what he had not said. In a short time she got used to his cock, enjoying getting to know his shape, the way her tongue bumped over the ridge that was the base of his tip. Pearl took him in hand again to keep him steady and give her more control. As she sucked upward, she moved her hand to follow her mouth, not knowing where she had gained the knowledge to do so but following her instincts. His cock throbbed, expanded somewhat, and each time she reached the tip she tasted that wonderful taste.

If this was the fluid Elizabeth had proclaimed ghastly, Pearl had to imagine how their perception of this act could be so different. Was Pearl a dirty girl underneath it all? Was she like those whores at the club, wanting nothing but to please men and suck them? This act pleased her more than she suspected it should, and before she went on to talk herself out of what she was doing, she shut away her thoughts. Time enough to ponder them later, when guilt arrived and shame burned her cheeks.

But I do not feel shame. I feel…powerful. This feels right.

James's fingers tightened in her hair, and he gripped her

shoulder as his length pulsated in her mouth. She bobbed her head faster, loving how he hardened more, how she knew to quicken her pace. It seemed natural, this taking of him in her mouth. Her cunt clenched and her bud ached, nipples hardening and brushing against her nightgown. Goose-bumps peppered her skin, spreading up her arms and down her back, their journey ending at the sensitive spot between her legs. She shivered, the sensation pleasurable, and itched to have his mouth there again, his tongue licking her as she licked him. Was that possible?

She drew up and he left her mouth with a soft pop. Full of desire she breathed out, "I want…I want you to lick me again while I lick you."

James caressed her face and brought her level with him, taking her mouth in a hard yet sensual kiss. Her heart rate increased until she swore the thrum of its beat filled the room. So many emotions and sensations overtook her that she pulled her mouth away, struggling to breathe and make sense of each feeling. She rested her forehead to his and spied his erection. It bobbed as though straining for her touch, her mouth, and she grasped him again, stroking his length with a tighter grip.

"Oh, God, Pearl…"

James lifted her nightgown, its rise demanding that she let go of the hardness she had quickly grown to want permanently in her hand. The feel of it was so novel that she knew she could play with it all night. She lifted her arms, and James took the nightgown off her body, the soft fabric whispering over her sensitised skin.

James tossed it on to the bed and surveyed her with what she surmised was need in his eyes. She did not feel embarrassed beneath his gaze, but liberated that he looked upon her as though she was the most beautiful thing he had ever seen. How was it that one look said so much? How was it that she knew what he was saying without him uttering a word? Her nipples hardened some more in the cooler air, and that same air swirled through the space between her inner thighs and emphasised the fact she was wet. Lord, she was wet.

She reached up and unbuttoned his shirt, frantic to remove it. She wanted to see him as he saw her, naked, exposed for her perusal. His shirt joined her nightshirt on the bed, and she tackled his lower garments, helping him take them off. He kneeled before her like a carved statue she had once seen, and the beauty that was his body took her breath away.

He cupped her face with both hands. "You are so beautiful, Pearl. I am so lucky to be here. That you want me this way."

Did she spy moisture in his eyes? He caressed her cheek with his thumbs, his touch so soft it brought a lump to her throat. Could she dare hope this was more than she had thought? That he had begun to care for her? It was not possible — no, it was not how things worked in Pearl's world.

He guided her on to the bed, settling onto his back as she kneeled beside him, her hand in his. She gazed at his body, taking him in from head to toe and back again. The male form was such a wonder to see, his shape so different from hers. His nipples stood up, a smattering of hair layering the valley between them, and she wondered how those tiny nubs would feel against her tongue. She bent and licked before she had the chance to change her mind. The soft contact did strange things to her, sending a skittering thrill across her skin and a more striking one between her legs. She licked his nipple again then raised her head to look at his face, tilting her head in question as to what she must do next.

"Climb onto me, but face my feet," he said, voice hoarse.

She frowned a little but complied, shifting around and lifting one leg to plant her knees either side of his waist. Their skin connected, and the sensations from that and the fact that her bottom faced him, exposed for his intimate perusal, sent a shocking dash of excitement through her. What they were doing was so…wrong.

No, it is not. How can something that feels so right be wrong?

She shook off her morals and once again pledged to enjoy the moment. Feelings like this may never come her way again.

"You will need to shift backwards, my love," he said.

My love!

Her heart soared, and she glanced back at him. Surely he would not enjoy her bottom closer than it already was?

"So I can lick you, Pearl."

She turned and faced the door, took in a deep breath, and shuffled in reverse so the backs of her knees sat snugly beneath his armpits. His warm breath heated her slit, and she shuddered with desire.

"Now lower yourself a little."

She did so, his breath hotter now, and held hers in anticipation of his next command.

"Lean down and suck my cock."

Eagerly she obeyed, drawing him inside her mouth, finding it easier to suck him from this angle. She circled her thumb and finger around his base and plunged down. His tip skated across the roof of her mouth until it reached the back of her throat, and she withdrew, sucking hard, a drop of his liquid spreading on her tongue. She knew at some point more fluid would seep from him, Elizabeth had said so, and she wondered whether it was proper to allow it to fill her mouth. Whether it was or not, she wanted to try. Sucking harder, faster, she listened to his stuttered groans and felt him pulse.

He lifted his hands and laid them on the sides of her thighs, fingertips pressing gently.

Then his tongue invaded her folds. She gasped on an upstroke of his cock, shocked at his sudden intrusion yet understanding how they could both pleasure the other at the same time. The combination of him licking her and her sucking him almost sent her insane. The intensity of those feelings grew to such proportions that her head lightened for a moment, leaving her feeling as though she might faint.

Pearl sucked and licked, while James's tongue and mouth worked magic on her wet slit.

It was too much. The burning, exquisite joy she had felt when he had licked her before came again, strong and fast, making her suck him quicker as her excitement built and exploded in a wave of euphoric bliss. Her hips jolted of their own accord, and she moaned, the sound buried in her throat along with the head of his cock.

His length pulsed on her tongue, and as she rocked back and forth over his mouth, that liquid she had been curious about spilled from him. It filled her mouth, and for a second she panicked, her first instinct to lift her head and remove him. Another spurt came, and she swallowed, feeling her execution was awkward as her mind struggled to process swallowing and sucking at the same time. But she managed, swallowing again and sucking him as though she had much practice in the past.

James groaned, the sound humming between her legs, joining the aftermath of her pleasure still radiating there. She drew up his length once his emissions stopped and took her mouth from him, lifting her chin so she stared at the ceiling. Her heart beat so wildly, the throb of her nub just as fierce, and she breathed through her nose in order to calm herself.

His mouth left her cunt, and he whispered, "Pearl, come here."

She turned and manoeuvred to lay beside him, embraced by his muscular arm. He trailed his fingertips up and down her back, and she rested her cheek to his chest, studying the fine hairs there to occupy her mind, which now raced. Embarrassment suddenly arrived, a hot blush to her cheeks. How must her bottom have looked presented to him that way?

"You are so beautiful. So wonderful," he murmured, raising his free hand to toy with her hair. "I do not think I could ever tire of you."

"Surely you will," she whispered, growing bold again,

enough to play with the hairs on his chest.

"I will not. And I shall return to ask permission to court you." He took his hand from her hair and slid a finger beneath her chin, lifting her face so she looked up at him. "I will not let you go now, Pearl."

Did he mean what she hoped? That she was his now?

Tears pricked the backs of her eyes, the abrupt sting near painful levels. She willed them not to fall, willed herself not to appear the lonely woman she really was. James seemed the kind of man who needed a strong woman by his side, not one like herself. She smiled and he kissed her brow, brushing a thumb over her lips. What she would give to have him in her bed for all time. In her life.

Was she enough for him? Could she dare to hope he meant what he had said?

"I can only pray you stick to your word and ask my aunt if she will allow you to court me. And I want you to return here tomorrow night, so we can..."

I sound so needy and have allowed him to see how much I want him. How much it will crush me if he is just playing with me and intends to let me down.

"You do not need prayers, Pearl. I will arrive to see your aunt as promised, have no fear that I will not. And I will most certainly return tomorrow at midnight. How can I not when you have buried yourself right under my skin?" He kissed her forehead again.

Had she done that? Really? Oh, he had said he had wanted to court her for some time, but the words could just be something he said in order to end up in her bed. And if they were, so be it. She refused to ponder the subject now. Time enough for looking back on this night in the future. And if he stuck to his word, she could look back on tomorrow night too.

She closed her eyes and snuggled into his chest, soaking up the feelings he inspired. To rest like this, in a man's arms, had been her wish for the longest time. That her dreams had come true was still something she had yet to believe.

It was almost as though she had dreamed their coupling...
that she still dreamed now.

Chapter Nine

The Diary of Seth Adams

November 10th, 11th, 1888

I had spent the day wanting to return to Pearl, to visit her aunt and request permission to court her niece. Her admission that the madam had coerced her into watching a sexual act had shocked me. I would have to have words with the woman and make it clear that those who worked downstairs did not wish to work upstairs. Prostitution was not for every woman, and the madam should have had the sense to know that. Still, I could not help but silently thank the woman, for she had drawn the vixen out in Pearl and given me a pleasurable night to remember.

The thought of my licking Pearl and her sucking my cock made me want to abandon what I was doing and visit her right away. Alas, some brewery matters needed my attention, and the morning passed in a blur of me rushing from one query to the next. I did not find time to eat lunch until well into late afternoon, and I sat in my office to indulge in a ham sandwich and a helping of pickles. A sweet cup of tea steaming in my hand, I settled back in my chair and propped my feet on the desk. The lack of sleep had begun to take its toll on my body – I had remained awake, watching Pearl as she slept in my arms – yet my mind remained alert. With the memories of Pearl swirling, it seemed she was all I needed to stay awake, the promise of my visit to her tonight an enticement that wiped away any desire to sleep.

I sipped my tea and thought about her, recalling her

scent and how her folds had felt upon my tongue. And her mouth on my cock…I had never experienced something so thrilling. What was it about her that set her apart from all the other women? She was a beauty, no doubt about that, but there was something else I could not quite put my finger on. I admitted that some souls belonged together, and no amount of explanation as to why mattered.

Placing my teacup on the desk, I reached for the newspaper, the early evening edition delivered by the young boy who dropped them off every weekday. He clearly lived in poverty and worked to supplement his parents' wages, so I tipped him heavily every Friday, the least I could do. I wanted so much to help the lower classes and vowed to look into how I could go about that without causing offence. They were a proud lot, the underprivileged Londoners.

The front page of the newspaper had me sitting bolt upright, my feet firmly planted on the floor. My heart thumped hard and fast, and I swallowed bile. There was more information on the latest murder, that of Mary Jane Kelly, in the early hours of yesterday morning. My mind flitted back to the fellow who had accosted Pearl outside the club, and my blood ran cold. Something about Percival Sloker bothered me, and I could not shake the feeling that there was more to him than met the eye. Had I not spoken to him before, it would be ludicrous of me to think he was the killer of prostitutes, yet… Was it really ludicrous? After all, he was in my club, perhaps looking for a victim, and what he had said in the alley was not something a man with nothing to hide would say. He had all but admitted his guilt, God damn him!

I frowned at my thoughts. I had nothing to base my assumption on except for his words. There were many men in the club that night. By rights, I should suspect them all. If the club was not situated so close to the murder sites, maybe I would not even think twice about Mr Sloker, but he was not a nice man, that was obvious.

But what if it *was* him?

A shiver rattled my spine, and I read the article with much interest. The poor woman had seemingly returned home as usual after a night out, placing her clothes in a folded pile on a chair and her boots in front of the fireplace. Her killer had called, possibly after she had retired to bed, and she was found by her rent collector, one Thomas Bowyer, who had peered through the window upon receiving no response from his knocks. Who on earth was this killer? And why was he targeting prostitutes?

I jumped from my seat and walked out of my office, intending to leave the locking up of the brewery to Kenneth. I had the urge to get to my club, and quickly. If anyone knew of any fresh gossip, John Robins would. I arrived there around six to find John once again polishing glasses, readying the club for the coming night's business. He poured me a whisky — my God, I needed it after reading the paper — and quirked a brow in question.

"John, what have you heard about this latest murder?" I sipped the whisky, its burn chasing away the chills.

He picked up another glass and absently polished it. "Ah, nasty business again, sir. Word is that the killer really went to town on this one. I knew Mary, you know. Nice woman, if a bit brash."

"So what have you heard?" I bit back a nugget of irritation that threatened to spill via harsh words. John's lack of haste in telling me the details had me tapping my foot in frustration.

"Ah." He stared into the middle distance. "People reckon she let the killer in. Poor cow probably thought he was a customer. He hacked her until she was unrecognisable. Yep, nasty business." John placed the glass on the shelf and selected another. "He cut off her breasts, sliced off her face, and one fella said she'd had her neck slit to the point the knife went right into the bone." He winced and cleared his throat.

"A strong man, then, the killer."

"Yep. He needs locking up."

I felt that was rather an understatement but refrained from voicing my thoughts. "John, that fellow in here…Percival Sloker. I went and found him in one of the public houses. Spoke to him. He is somewhat, dare I say it, frightening. I am not afraid of any man, but him? He is strange, has an air about him that I do not trust or like, and I am unsure what to do about it."

John paused in polishing. "What is there to do about it except rough him up a bit?"

"He may as well have admitted to being the killer, John."

"What? Are you saying what I think you are? That you reckon he has something to do with…" He shook his head. "You sound as mad as the killer is, sir."

"That is as may be, but what if I am right? Could I continue as though oblivious, when I have thoughts such as these running through my head? Women's lives are at stake here!" I gulped the remainder of my whisky, slammed the glass down, and pushed away from the bar. I knew I sounded irrational, yet my blood was up and my instincts were screaming. How could I explain that to another? How could I tell someone that just by being in that wretched man's company, I sensed a darkness in him so deep and ingrained that, even if he was not the killer, I knew he was up to something sinister.

"We all think that way, sir." John dampened a cloth and cleaned the bar top in wide, circular swipes. "But the killer… he is something entirely different to that fella. Sloker is just a strange man, nothing more or less." He turned to the wall behind the bar and wiped over a brandy bottle.

I eyed in him the mirror. He appeared to be mulling something over.

He lifted his gaze and met mine. "He near enough admitted to killing, you say?"

"He implied as much. He was arrogant and full of himself. He drew a knife on me."

John turned to face me. "Oh, well, that gives things a

different slant, sir. What happened?"

"I punched him."

John chuckled. "No more than he deserved, what with him pulling the knife."

"I did not have — *do* not have — any basis for my suspicions other than a feeling deep in my gut. That and what he said. I cannot, in all good conscience, let the matter drop."

"Then seek him out again, sir. Question him. And if he gives insufficient answers, visit the law. They are having the devil of a time trying to find the killer. If it *is* Sloker…"

I thought about that for a moment, pinching my chin between finger and thumb. "Yes, you are right. What harm can it do to speak to him again, speak to the authorities? If it comes to nothing, if Sloker has an alibi, there will have been no harm done."

"And then you can sleep at night."

I almost chuckled. I would not be sleeping much at night if Pearl insisted I visit her in the dark hours again. Nodding, I walked towards the door. "I shall try and find him now."

"Take care, sir."

"I will."

I left the club and made my way to the public house Sloker had been in before. On the way, I questioned my sanity. The man was clearly dangerous, possibly deranged if he carried a knife about his person, and I was intent on confronting him. Why was I doing such a thing? I clenched my teeth, knowing full well the answer to that question. Sloker's implied threat to Pearl had buried under my skin, caused an itch I could not scratch unless I secured her safety once and for all. And what did I mean by that?

I did not answer myself, instead walking into the bar and ordering another whisky. Pipe smoke loitered just below the ceiling, the stench of it heavy in my nostrils. People of varying levels of lower class sat around scarred tables, playing cards or conversing in loud, eardrum-grating voices. I lifted my drink, planned to sip it for an hour or two, and if Sloker did not appear, I would go home for a time to bathe then take the carriage to visit Pearl. I did not want to remain any longer than necessary.

The minutes seeped past. The clock behind the bar read eight o'clock by the time I swallowed the last of my drink. I contemplated ordering another, but that would make three whiskeys this night and I did not want to be a drunken oaf when I arrived at Pearl's. The door to the street pushed open, and I started in response, hoping Sloker would enter. He did not. Perhaps he had taken my warning to heart and would keep away from the area. Also, would he venture out after killing so recently?

Stop it, man. He may not even be the damn killer.

I left the pub telling myself I had at least tried to find him. All I could do now was keep my eyes and ears open and ensure Pearl remained safe. How I would do the latter when she lived so out of the way I did not know. Maybe she would not be averse to a suggestion about a male employee living on the premises. The thought of two women alone in that house, with only the occasional visit by the maid, did not sit easily in my mind.

Once home and in my room, I bathed, shaved, and pondered on whether to let a beard or moustache grow, but I had never been one for facial hair and Pearl had been attracted to me without it. God forbid I do anything to change her feelings towards me — I must keep her interest in me intact. The thought of losing her entered my mind then, and I shrugged such musings away, only for them to return with taunts about my not disclosing my true identity.

I must tell her tonight, before she finds out for herself.

The clock seemed to tick with interminable slowness, and by the time eleven o'clock arrived, I was nervous and jumpy. If I took the carriage at a leisurely pace, I could arrive at Pearl's just before midnight. How I longed to see her waiting at the window, to see her face once more as she gazed down into the garden.

Doubts crept in. Would she still feel the same? Since I last saw her, she had had time to think about her actions. Lust and desire did things to a body, lent a different perspective to a person's thoughts. Perhaps the stark light of a new day had changed her view of me, reminding her that what we had done was against society's rules.

Damn! If we were married…

But I could not marry her unless she agreed.

Unless I tell her the truth.

I gathered my resolve and left the house, forgetting to keep the horse at a casual trot. I arrived at Pearl's a little after eleven-thirty and left my carriage on the road, hidden by the bushes and trees at the edge of her property. I tied the horse's reins to a branch and hoped no one would happen by, scare the beast or take note that a late-night visitor had called at the house. Pearl did not deserve the scandal.

Taking a deep breath, I glanced at her home in the near distance. All the lights were doused, and I stepped onto the driveway, intent on walking slowly to kill some time. A shuffling of leaves had me spinning to face the road. There was no wind, no reason other than an animal foraging to have created that noise, and my heart rate sped. I squinted, gaze darting left and right to catch sight of whatever was there, seeing nothing but the silhouettes of tree trunks, knobbly and misshapen.

I waited a moment then turned back to face the house. I had the jitters, that was all, and began the long walk up the drive. The shuffle sounded again, and I jerked my head to the side a second before a blow struck the base of my skull. Pain bloomed, and I lurched forward, hands outstretched to break my fall. I was aware of movement behind me as I landed on the gravel, the small stones biting into my palms, and I rolled onto my back to get a good look at my assailant.

My God, I knew I was right about him. Sloker stood over me, cosh in hand, a menacing look upon his face. His cape fell forward about his sides, his hat shadowed his face, and he leant down to peer at me through slitted eyes. I scrabbled backward, incensed he was there, that he had the audacity to make good his threat.

What kind of man was he, that he would make enquiries as to Pearl's identity and her location? Or had he followed me the previous night, pretending to be unconscious on the cobbles after I had struck him? If it was the former, he knew Pearl's true name. As far as I knew, only Frances and I knew Pearl had been at the club. Everyone else knew her as Lily.

My thoughts spun out of control, and I leapt to my feet, lunging at him, shoving my hands against his chest and pushing him backward.

He was strong, I would give him that, and it reminded me of the force used on Mary Jane Kelly's neck. He merely staggered, righting himself in no time. An angry growl grew inside me, spewing from my mouth as I shoved him again. He laughed, unsteady on his feet for only a second, and raised the cosh. It came down as though time had slowed. I stared at its arc before scooting to the side and kicking him in the bollocks. He grunted, doubled over, then stood upright so quickly it took me off guard.

The cosh caught me on the jaw, the pain so intense I shouted out. Anger boiled inside me – damned if I would let him beat me so he could reach Pearl – and I forged forward, grabbing the hair at his temples. His hat flew off, and I brought his face down onto my raised knee, satisfied at hearing a loud crack. He howled and raised his hands, grasping my wrists and throwing me off him. Blood streamed from his nose, tears pooled in his eyes, and he shook his head. Despite his obvious disorientation, he raised the cosh again. Luck was on his side as to my whereabouts, and the cosh came down towards my head. I jumped back, landing a fist in his gut and following through with another to his jaw.

"You bastard!" he ground out, clenching his teeth. His breath left him in gusty pants. Once more he attacked, a smirk skewing his lips so the blood's course diverted into the grooves either side.

I hit him again, an uppercut to his chin, and this time he fell backward, swept off his feet by the force of the blow.

He landed heavily, air pushing out between his lips, but struggled to his feet.

I held my fists at my sides. "You had better get the hell away from here, or so help me God—"

"He will not help you." Sloker laughed, a sinister, cold cackle that chilled my blood.

His cavalier attitude and reason for being here incensed me. I reached out and grabbed his cloak, hauling him upright and forcing him to walk towards the road. He pushed against me, flailed his arms in an attempt to strike, but my speed and momentum prevented it.

"Those women," I said, voice low and hard. "Was it you?"

Sloker smiled, teeth discoloured with blood, and again tried to squirm out of my grip. "They are an abomination, a stain on the world, and they need eradicating. They deserved everything they got."

He had not answered my question, and I repeated it.

"Yes!" he hissed. "And I will get them all."

My stomach bunched at his admission. I was right, and although I gained some satisfaction from my instincts being true, I was not sure what to do. This man would not allow me to take him back to the city and hand him over to the police. I would have to knock him out in order to ensure he remained in my carriage. The thought of what he had done to those poor women came to mind and, on the road, I flung him away from me with a growl, unable to bear touching him any longer. He reeled backward, arms thrashing as his body smacked into the ground and the cosh sailed into a ditch.

He did not move.

Irate as I was, the understanding that something bad had happened filtered through me. My heart worked harder to keep up with the shock, and a tinge of fear crept into my innards. Walking to him, I wondered if he was playing dead, whether he would jump up once I was close enough for him to grab hold of me and drag me to the ground. I toed his leg, waiting for some response, but he remained inert, eyes open and staring at the blackness above. A forbidding chill gripped me then, and I went down on my knees to shake the man into coming to. A sharp rock beneath his head must have pierced his skull, and those open eyes and lack of breath told me the terrible truth.

I had killed a man. Albeit a murderer, but I had taken a life just the same.

Panic began as a hollowing of my stomach at first, then grew in intensity as it flooded my body. Weak and nauseated, for a moment I remained on my knees trying to work out what I should do next. Fear combined with the panic. Would the police believe my tale? That this was the man who had butchered women for doing nothing but sharing their body in order to survive? Did I have enough standing in society for them to take my word that Sloker had admitted to being the monster who was Jack the Ripper?

And what of Pearl? She would find out who I was through other sources and associate me with yet another death. I stood and rubbed my chin, looking at her house, working out my options.

Making a decision, I dragged Sloker to my carriage. He was a heavy bastard, and I had trouble putting him inside, but after much grappling I managed to complete the task. I unhitched my horse and climbed up, settling into the seat. I set the animal at a steady pace and headed for the city. On the way, so very conscious that a dead man lay sprawled across my carriage seat, I thought of a suitable place to take him and reasoned that a terrible human being had been prevented from killing anyone ever again.

But would my conscience rest easy with the knowledge that I had killed him?

On the outskirts, I spotted the perfect place and urged my horse to a stop beside a field. A ditch ran between that and the road, and I alighted, opening the carriage door with my mind on the task ahead.

Sloker was sitting up.

I almost barked out a curse in fright but quelled it just

in time. Feigning nonchalance, I said, "I am taking you to the authorities." I stepped back from the door, preparing myself to hit Sloker once more, hard enough to knock him senseless, giving me time to get him to the law.

He lunged forward, fell out of the carriage onto the road, eyes glazed, and stared around, clearly confused. I readied myself for another attack, but Sloker merely stared at me, falling to his knees, arms raised to the heavens. He pitched forward, rolling onto his side. His body stilled, and I hunkered down to check for a pulse. I could not detect one.

I have nothing to rebuke myself for. If he is dead now, I did not kill him.

Before I could change my mind, I climbed aboard and clucked my horse into action, guiding him around Sloker so I could travel back the way I had come. I would go and visit Pearl, then, come morning, ride back this way and happen upon his body. I would report to the law that I had found him on the road on my way into the brewery, that he must have wandered out here and fallen, died from his head striking the ground. Relief at him being dead made my hands shake, and as the carriage moved away, I glanced back.

He still lay where I had left him.

I arrived at Pearl's just after half past midnight. As before, I secured my horse, but this time I rushed up the driveway. She would have been waiting for half an hour at the window, and the thought of her thinking I was not going to appear hurt my heart. As I veered across the grass to go around the back of the house, the front door opened and her slender figure stood in the doorway. Such a force of love took hold of me that I had to stop myself from racing towards her and sweeping her into my arms. She appeared relieved and smiled, lifting one finger to her lips and beckoning me inside.

This night would not be a happy one, so I took a moment to drink in the sight of her, for I had the ominous feeling she would not want to see me again once I confessed who I was.

A lump pained my throat, and I smiled, determined not to alert her just yet that something was wrong. I followed her upstairs and into her room, the scent of her swallowing me whole.

She locked the door and stepped into my arms, pressing her cheek to my chest. I held her there, closing my eyes to better etch this feeling into my memory, and brushed my lips across the top of her head. It would be lonely without her. No, worse than that—desolate, unbearable, but I had to tell her the truth.

Pearl lifted her chin and looked up at me, her beautiful eyes and curved mouth striking a chord deep inside me. By God, she was so pretty, so delightful, and the feel of her in my arms was almost too much to bear.

"I could not wait for you to come," she whispered, raising a hand and tracing my lips with a fingertip. "When you were late I thought..." She sighed. "I thought you would not come. I missed you today, sweet James."

Her use of my middle name burned. "Pearl, there is something I must tell you."

"Of course," she said, leading me to the bed. She sat, pulling me down beside her. "You can tell me anything."

Anything? Oh no, my sweet, I cannot, but I must.

I cleared my throat and pushed on before I could change my mind. "My name is not James. It is Seth—Seth Adams."

126

Chapter Ten

November 11th, 1888

Pearl widened her eyes and stared at James in shock. Had she heard him correctly? He was Seth Adams, the one who had championed the man responsible for her parents' deaths? She eased her body away from him, although her thigh still pressed against his. Her mind had trouble believing that the man who sat beside her was the same one she had wondered about for so long. And he did not look as she had imagined. The Seth of her mind was ugly, with cold eyes and an evil sneer. Not this man, not James, who gazed at her, his features etched with pain.

"I..." She stood and walked to the door, fingers poised over the key. She should ask him to leave, never to return, but the tales her aunt had told her about him did not tally with the man she so far knew him to be.

Her aunt had been passionate that Seth Adams had supported his employee, but Pearl had thought privately that her father's death had been an accident. No man of good standing championed a killer, she knew that, and her aunt's ramblings had mainly gone ignored by Pearl as the rants of a woman demented by grief at losing her brother.

How could Pearl turn him away now? She rested her forehead on the door and inhaled deeply. How could she never see him again after what they had done? After what he had made her feel? Like a foolish young girl, she had allowed herself to fall in love with him quickly, and the knowledge brought her up short.

I am in love with a man my aunt expects me to detest.

Far from feeling repulsed at Seth standing up for his employee, she admired him. If she loved him, would that not transcend all issues? She would listen to his explanation. What harm could that do?

None, except bring back the pain of Mother's and Father's passing, and I do not want…I cannot bring myself to relive it all over again. What he did does not matter – only to my aunt.

"Pearl, it is not how you think. Your parents' deaths…the man—"

"Please, just…just be quiet for a moment." She raised her hand to prevent him speaking again and listened for signs that he was leaving the bed to come to her. She could not stand that if he did. Not right now, not when she needed a few minutes to tell herself what she knew she must do – go against her aunt and be with her man.

Frances's earlier visit came back with startling clarity. She had come for afternoon tea, had tried to tell Pearl who James— *Seth, will I ever get used to calling him that?* —was by saying, "You must be careful regarding him, Pearl…"

Pearl had taken it as sour grapes that she had acted the harlot and Frances had not. Would Pearl have felt differently about James if Frances had spelled out the truth? Would she have allowed him to visit this night? To enter her home?

Yes, I would. He has worked his way inside me, and I cannot deny him.

With a sigh, she faced him, pressing her back to the door. He looked at her with such sorrow she was hard pressed not to run to him and bury herself in his arms. Lines had appeared beside his mouth, and deep furrows marred his brow. What was he thinking?

Pearl thought she knew but asked, "Why did you tell me now? Why wait until after…" She twisted her fingers together and waited for what seemed an interminably long time for his answer.

"I…" He stood and lifted his arms then dropped them by his sides. "I thought if you knew from the start you would not have given me a chance. I heard that you detested me."

"I have never said such a thing. It is my aunt who detests you."

He seemed shocked at that. "Oh. I was told... It does not matter what I was told. Before this...we...go any further, I thought it best you should know the truth. In case you do not wish me in your life now...let it be said that I would be devastated." He gazed at her, a silent plea for her understanding. "I have kept my distance for a long time, Pearl. Seeing you in the club seemed like fate. That we were meant to be together. It sounds foolish, I know, but-"

"I feel the same way." Compassion flooded her at the relief on his face. She slowly walked towards him and, with mere inches between them, raised her hand to stroke his face. "I have no reason to hate you. My father's death was an accident. If I believed my aunt I would ask you to leave, but I will not. I should do many things...and also should not have done many things, but I have and I do not regret them." She paused. "I do not regret you."

She stood on tiptoes and closed her eyes, waiting for his lips to meet hers. They did not, and she lifted her lashes. Panic that he had changed his mind about her made her giddy, and she cocked her head, searching for answers in his eyes.

Abruptly, he held the back of her head and crushed his mouth to hers. He slid his tongue inside and settled his other hand on her bottom, pressing her to his erection. Her head whirled, and her knees weakened at the intimate contact, and Lord, she wanted him inside her, to feel his body over hers.

James eased away and looked at her. "I take it that you are willing to listen to my side?"

"If you wish to tell it, but not now. Now, I want...you. All of you."

He raised his eyebrows and widened his eyes. "Pearl, I am not sure we—"

"But I am." *God, I am.*

"What...how do you feel? What do you want?" He took

his hand from her hair and ran the back of his finger down her cheek.

"I want you inside me."

Lord, did I say that aloud? By the shock on his face, she had.

"Pearl… I want the same, believe me, but there are things we must discuss. Things I want you to understand. Not just about the past but now and the future."

She boldly smoothed her hands up his back and held him closer, pressing his chest to her breasts. "Tell me about now. The past is…the past, and the future is obvious to me."

"But it is not to me. What do you see?"

"I cannot explain why, nor how my feelings for you have developed so rapidly, but the future… I am here if you will have me. A gentleman's harlot."

Because you will not want me as your wife – you are surely too sought after by other, prettier women to want me that way.

"A gentleman's harlot? But I had hoped for so much more than that, Pearl." He stroked her face again. "I had hoped… Do you see me only as a plaything? Someone to pass the nighttime with? Someone to teach you how a man likes to be pleasured?"

Do I admit how I feel? What I really want? Will my aunt even allow him to court me when she sees who has come to ask her permission?

She took a deep breath. "What I want I do not always get. I have learned to live with disappointment and loneliness. I have low expectations, for then I am not crushed when my dreams do not come true." Tears pricked her eyes, and she lowered her gaze so he would not see them fall.

"Tell me. I need to know if we want the same thing." He kissed her, a soft touch of his lips.

"I want…you. Marriage, children, the whole unattainable dream." Pearl laughed quietly, hearing his answer in her mind, repeating it so when he uttered the words they would not sting as much.

"Then we want the same thing."

Pearl snapped her head back up to face him, her heart

hammering fast and strong. "We do?" She held her breath.

Things like this do not happen to me. Beautiful men like this do not want a redhead who knows nothing of how things work in the real world.

"Yes, we do, and I want my unattainable dream with you."

"Then they are not unattainable if they are there for the taking," she murmured, in shock, feeling as though she dreamed and that any second fate would be cruel and wake her up. She smiled, still unable to believe this was happening but enjoying the emotions filling her. The past could wait—she had meant that, it was not important now—and the future, that beautiful future she had longed for appeared to be stretching before her, but the now...

No, that could *not* wait. Her wanton side rose within her, pushing her to say, "If you wish to marry me, sir, it would not matter if you took me now. I was truthful in what I said, but in case you did not hear me correctly, I shall repeat it." She licked her lips, held him tighter, and her nipples hardened. "I want you. All of you."

He pounced, claiming her mouth in a hot and frantic kiss, the breaths from his nose whispering across her face. She delighted in his hands roaming up and down her back then pressing into her shoulder blades so she was clamped against him, held tighter than she had ever been. His fingertips dug into her, and his elbows nestled at her waist, cocooning her in an embrace so solid that if he let her go she would slump to the floor.

She had grown weak, her legs surely unable to support her, and her pulse thudded so hard in her throat that it bordered on pain. Her Adam's apple seemed to harden, cutting off her air supply, and a strangled groan pushed to be set free. Managing to suck in a breath, she returned the kiss, her tongue meshing with his, the sensations produced so erotic she feared a faint.

He must have sensed her struggling to compose herself for he dragged his mouth from hers and brushed his lips across her cheek, along her jawline, and down her arched neck. She took the opportunity to regain control of her senses, clutching at his back then curling her fingers over his shoulders as though he were a lifeline. And he was, was he not? Her anchor at this time, the one who was steady and knowing while she floundered, ignorant of what would happen next.

Oh, she had discussed such things with Frances, but neither of them had understood how it would be until Elizabeth had given them her version of the truth. Pearl had certainly not realised that a mere kiss could steal her breath and leave her so weak.

"You are so beautiful," he said against her neck, his words hot on her skin. "I want you in my life — in my bed — forever."

She closed her eyes as the sting of tears came, then held him tighter. Had someone really said that to her? Did this man mean that? Forever was a long time. Surely one such as him would tire of her. She was so ordinary, so dull.

"You are the most exquisite creature I have ever met, Pearl. I have loved you for such a long time."

He trailed his tongue up her neck and to her ear, suckling the lobe and sending tendrils of pleasure down to her… *cunt, to my wet and ready cunt…*

"Oh, God," she breathed, the words she had thought bringing on a stronger wave of desire. She was dizzy with a need, one she recognised now as lust, although she had no solid idea of what to do. Her mind was unversed in an experience such as this, yet her body… Yes, she would do what she did before and let her body direct itself, allow instinct to take over and lead the way.

He lifted his head, and the loss of his mouth on her earlobe left it cold and her wanting more. She opened her eyes to find him staring at her, his eyes soft and shrouded in what she could only guess was desire. How she had dreamed of a man looking at her this way, with utter adoration, as though she were the most beautiful woman on Earth. And with his study came the feeling that at this moment in time she *was* beautiful. To feel so wanted, so special, had her fighting tears away.

"Pearl, is something wrong?" He gathered her closer still, cradling the back of her head with one hand.

"No," she said, that one word breathy and so quiet she worried he had not heard her. "No, nothing is wrong. Everything is so…right."

He pressed his lips to her forehead, and her mouth was so close to his neck she wondered if she had the nerve to dash out her tongue and taste his skin. It was such a bold thing to do, but her audacity had deserted her tonight. Had she used up all her courage by telling him she wanted him inside her? What had happened to the woman she had been with him before, the one who appeared in control and knew what she wanted?

We were playing games then. I had not thought for one minute he was serious, that he had the same dreams as I. And now…now it is real and I do not want it to go awry. She swallowed as his hands smoothed down her back to caress the globes of her bottom. *Now I am afraid of losing him.* He squeezed her flesh, and a ripple of want warmed her cunt. *Now I am afraid that I will wake up and find myself alone again, with only the memories of my dream to keep me company.*

A sudden and fierce longing to keep him close took over her, and she flashed her tongue out, the tip meeting with his hot skin. He tasted salty and like nothing she had ever tasted before, a tang for which she had no name, but loved nevertheless.

Seth groaned, the vibration humming through her tongue, and she mewled, her knees jolting. He held her steady, and while she retracted her tongue and fought for breath, he rested his cheek to the top of her head and cradled her. They stood for what seemed an eternity, Pearl cloaked in safety and the feeling of being completely protected. How had she gone so long without this?

"We do not need to go further if you would rather not,"

he said, raising one hand so his fingertips massaged her scalp, his other hand splayed in the centre of her back.

She nestled her head in the crook of his shoulder, her lips close to the neck she wanted to taste again—taste more fully. Relaxing, she let her hands trail down his back to *his* bottom and mirrored what he had done to hers. His taut flesh gave a little beneath her touch, and she took a few moments to learn the shape of him, to explore the way his back met with his bottom and how the curves tapered into the tops of his thighs. Her breaths were hot in such a confined space, bringing out his scent—woodsy, the hint of lavender, and an aroma she had smelt when he had been this close...before.

Her remaining silent and exploring his rear would surely answer him on whether she would like to go further. She did not trust herself to speak—a squeak was hardly romantic—and taking the time to investigate how he felt seemed natural and the right thing to do. His rear tightened beneath her touch, his muscles bunching with every stroke. Her cunt reacted in kind, muscles clenching and unclenching, making her bud throb so violently she sucked in a shocked breath. This would take some getting used to, this...this intimacy, but she wanted more of it, wanted to drown in him every time they were alone like this.

He slid one hand down her back to settle over the top of her bottom and suddenly pulled her into him. Her mound pressed against another hardness, a ridge she had sucked and licked and tasted. The memory of doing so infused her with the courage to cant her hips and shove into him. His rigidity abraded her needy nub, and his low moan had her stomach rolling over. God, how he affected her so!

Swiftly, he lifted her in his arms and gazed down at her. "By God, woman, I want you so much."

Pearl's stomach rolled again, and a breath caught in her throat. His gaze, it was so intense, so penetrating that she would swear she could read his mind. He *did* want her, as much as she wanted him, and she silently thanked him for

134

taking control. She did not have the ability to do so and wanted Seth to orchestrate how their first proper joining would be. Her need to be taken, pliant and willing beneath him, his strength and sexual knowledge overpowering her, would fit her ideal of how she had dreamed her marriage night would be. That maleness, that understanding he undoubtedly had of how to please a woman…she wanted it all, to be taken care of, to be told and shown and kissed and…fucked.

Fucked…

"Oh, God. I…please…" She snaked her hand to the nape of his neck and pulled his head towards hers. "Take me. Show me everything. Teach me how it is done."

He kissed her soundly, his lips firm, his tongue searching, and groaned as he snatched his mouth away to place her in the centre of the bed. She stared at him as he climbed on and loomed over her, his hands braced either side of her head, his knees digging into the mattress beside her outer thighs. She had the urge to widen her legs, to have him settle between them, and followed her instincts. Seth lifted one knee so she could ease her legs open then reached down and bunched her nightgown up around her waist. He moved and filled the space she had created, and oh, the cooler air kissing her pulsating slit was heaven.

He pushed her nightgown up farther, revealing her breasts. He bent to suckle one taut nipple. Pleasure radiated, spreading throughout her breast, and she arched her back a little so he sucked harder. A sound rumbled in his throat, and he glanced at her face as he swirled his tongue around, the look in his eye telling her he enjoyed every moment. He released her nipple, then claimed her lips. She reached between them as they kissed, freeing his cock and pushing his lower garments down his legs. She did not care that they were not naked—all she wanted was to have him inside her. Eager to feel his hard length in her hand, she grasped him, pleased at the sound of him inhaling sharply though his nose. He groaned, and she moved him so his tip butted her entrance.

James lifted his mouth from hers and looked down at her. "This will hurt, Pearl. There is nothing I can do to prevent that. And it may not feel good for you when I am inside this time. But it will get better, I promise, the more we practice."

She smiled despite anxiety unfurling deep in her belly, and recalled Elizabeth's lurid tale of how she had thought she was being ripped in two when her husband had penetrated her. Would it be that bad? Truly?

"Putting it off will not make it hurt any less. It will happen now. And like you said, we can practice until it does not hurt anymore." Her words belied the apprehension, which grew as she waited for him to push inside her. She was expecting a terrible amount of pain but there was no way she would not see this through. "Please, let us do this."

He gazed at her, his concern evident in his frown. "I will try to be as gentle as I can, my love."

Pearl looked up at him, fixing her gaze on his eyes, and felt the solid press of his tip seeking entrance. Just with him settled there like that she already felt full, his rounded end nestled at the rim of her channel, and she wondered how he would manage to fit inside. He lifted a hand to caress her cheek then pushed his cock in a little. It seemed as though he filled her already, yet she knew he did not. It was a foreign feeling, having something down there and inside her, all thickness and stretch, a sharp burn unlike anything she had felt before. She readied herself for the introduction of his full length. Hands on his back, she clutched his clothing in her fists and waited.

With gentle care, he breached her entrance, and she continued to stare up at him, holding her breath as she felt the stretch intensify. As he eased inside some more, she thought she had reached her limit, for the tight feeling of her sheath expanding to accommodate him bordered on pain. And then he gave a sharp, quick thrust, and real pain shot through her as she felt her maidenhood break. Heat radiated in her channel, and as James pushed further she gritted her teeth, holding back a cry as her body tried to resist his cock being there.

"I am so sorry," he said, dipping his head to pepper kisses across her mouth. "It may hurt some more when I move now."

She nodded, unable to trust herself to speak, and gripped the fabric in her fists tighter. She had so wanted to feel the wonderful bliss she had when James licked her, but tonight she knew it would not be that way. He moved carefully, and after several strokes the pain eased somewhat. She jerked her chin up, silently asking him to kiss her so she could lose herself in their lips joining rather than focusing on the tenderness below. It was not the kind of hurt Elizabeth had experienced, not enough to prevent Pearl from enjoying his tongue probing her mouth and his fingers tweaking her nipple.

He picked up speed, and their kiss deepened, taking Pearl to another level where the chafing in her sheath changed from uncomfortable to bearable. She felt him widen, felt the pulse of that vein she had licked the previous night throbbing against her inner walls. She wanted to raise her legs and wrap them around him but did not dare, fearful that the slight change in position might bring on more pain.

Blessed relief came, his passage easier, her body seeming to accept the foreign intrusion. She relaxed, surprised at how her channel adapted further with the loosening of her tense muscles. His pelvis abraded the nub between her legs, though not quite enough to give her the pleasure she had received before.

She took her mouth from his. "Touch my cunt. I need…"

He let go of her nipple and snaked his hand between them, raising his torso and holding himself away from her with his other hand flat to the bed. His questing thumb found her needy spot and rubbed, fast, circular movements that, coupled with his thrusts inside her, ratcheted up her excitement level. She strove for the release she had quickly come to crave and looked into his eyes as the pressure built.

She reached the crest and her enjoyment peaked, overflowing, filling her body with a rush of love, and as James quickened his pace, as his hot seed spurted, she rode out her pleasure with him, knowing without a doubt that yes, she would like to practice this often.

Chapter Eleven

The Diary of Seth Adams

November 11th, 1888

That Pearl wanted the same life as I — with me — was astounding. I had convinced myself that I would be saying goodbye, ousted from her home with a shove to my back and ordered never to return.

I left her house just before dawn, when the maid was due to arrive, and climbed aboard my carriage. My horse had fared well overnight and took off at a brisk trot. I would have him fed once we arrived home. On the first leg of my fog-laden journey, I worked through the flurry of thoughts congregating in my mind, all jostling to be heard first. I shook my head to clear it, but the questions persisted. While the crisp morning air shocked the residue of fatigue from my body, I snapped the reins and mulled over what my beautiful lady and I had discussed prior to my leaving. I would return to her house at lunchtime and present myself to her aunt.

I expected resistance from the older woman, but we must be married as soon as possible.

As I approached the stretch of road where I had left Percival Sloker, I narrowed my eyes in the gloom in hopes of seeing his body upon the ground. I admit I should not have wanted death for any human being, but given his past activities I assured myself that God would not hold my desires against me.

His body was not there.

Panic welled inside me. Had someone found him dead? *Or alive?* Had he merely been unconscious, able to rouse himself? I was not sure what to do and slowed my carriage in order to scour the ditch for sight of him. As far as I could tell in the poor lighting, Sloker was definitely not there. I turned in a circle, without a clue as to what I should do next. I had left Pearl's with plans to happen upon the body and visit the police station, but this turn of events changed matters.

I would have to wait and see what happened. If a report of a dead body appeared in the newspaper, giving firm evidence it was Sloker, I could rest easy without telling a soul of his confession to me. The murders would have died with him. But if no report came, he would be alive — although not well until he had recovered from the bumps and bruises I had given him — and able to kill again.

The idea of that soured my stomach.

Back aboard my carriage, I returned home to catch an hour or two of sleep before visiting the brewery. Sleep was not to be had, however, and I lay beneath the covers, my head full of Percival Sloker instead of my beautiful Pearl. There I remained, forgoing the visit to the brewery in favour of resting. I had not slept in too many hours to count, and although my mind and body flagged, I could not shut off and gain blessed respite.

Lunchtime drew near, and I left home with my stomach churning for other reasons. I would be seeing Pearl again, and once more trepidation at her having had time to rethink her decisions plagued me. What would I do if she had decided against our marriage while we had been apart?

It would kill me.

I steered the carriage up the driveway and alighted, knocking on the front door with my heart pattering too fast and my throat thickened from fear of the unknown. I had never asked for a woman's hand in marriage before, and although Pearl had assured me of her feelings, a small worm anticipating rejection wiggled inside me.

God, she has me at sixes and sevens.

The door opened and the maid stood in the threshold. She smiled and gestured that I should enter. The foyer smelt of beeswax and Pearl's unique scent. I glanced around in search of the lady who filled my heart. She stood in the drawing room with her back to me, pacing before the fireplace. A burgundy dress covered a body I had actually had the pleasure to touch, moulding to curves that had yielded beneath my hands. I still could not quite believe that all those nights of dreaming about her had become reality, and the realisation hit me full force.

My God, I love her.

She turned, her face lighting up as she took in the fact that I had come, and I knew then that she had entertained the same thoughts as I. We were a pair, and no mistake, both worrying needlessly. Perhaps we wanted our dreams so much that we still had doubts about receiving them so easily, that surely a cog would fail to work or a spring snap as the machine that was our plans worked harder.

"James," she whispered, raising a hand to her chest. "You are here." Still uncertainty lingered on her face, her eyes asking, "Are you here to see my aunt, or here to tell me you have changed your mind?"

I stepped into the living room, gaze fixed on her pretty face, the set of her hair as tresses cascaded from the curly nest atop her head. The redness of it should have clashed with her dress but it did not. Instead, it contrasted well, and despite how lovely she looked, I wanted to strip the fabric from her body and see that hair splayed against her creamy skin.

"I have come to speak with your aunt."

Her cheeks coloured a little, and she released a small gasp, darting her eyes sideward. I followed their journey, spying the elderly aunt sitting on the window seat gazing out at the front grounds. A grey day dress seemed to swamp her, and a black shawl not unlike those worn by common London women hugged her shoulders. Her hair had been styled into a knot at the nape of her neck, the colour the same grey as her dress. She looked unwell, her skin parchment thin and pale, and as she turned to face me with a faux smile I wondered if she was in pain and trying hard to disguise it.

"Mistress Lewis," I said, walking towards her and taking her hand in mine. I kissed the back of her hand then released it. "I trust I find you well?"

She sat up straighter and rolled her bony shoulders. "You have not, for I am in a quandary as to why it is *you* who has come to visit today. I thought it would be someone else. I had come to the conclusion that Pearl did not like you."

Pearl did not tell her it was I.

I swallowed and smiled. "I have settled any issues Pearl has with regard to my part in her past." A quick glance towards Pearl gave me the confidence to continue. "And I have come to ask for her hand in marriage."

The old woman glared at me, her eyes cold and her mouth set in a thin straight line. Her lips quivered, and she said, "It is all very well asking for her hand, but you have yet to *court* her. I have seen no evidence that you have done so, although there *is* evidence that you have been most improper. Do you not think it is better for Pearl that you make it known you have been visiting here for some time before you announce your plans to wed?"

"Of course," I said, smiling with as much warmth as I could manage. *She had not been asleep when I had visited after all.* "How much time would you require?"

She sucked in a long breath and released it slowly, rudely turning from me and looking back out the window. "Given the circumstances, you may wish to make it known you have already visited here *several* times immediately. I am not as deaf as *some* people may think."

A loud gasp from Pearl had me blushing for her, and I felt all manner of bastard that she had been placed in this position. I should have denied her requests, should have —

"So, then," the old woman said, "despite one of your employees killing my brother and you championing the brute, you should begin wedding arrangements as soon as possible. Perhaps being married within a month would be better. A child clearly conceived out of wedlock is not something I would relish explaining, although I hope to God above I will be long gone before then. To see my niece married to one such as you will get me to my grave faster."

I looked at Pearl, whose face and neck had reddened perceptibly. She wrung her hands, her eyes flicking side to side. I tried to convey my apologies to her with a glance I hoped showed my sorrow at her being in this position, and it seemed she understood my intent for she smiled and gave a slight nod.

"Very well." I cleared my throat. "I shall put word about and begin organising everything immediately. Thank you. Now, please may I take Pearl for a walk on the grounds?"

"You may," her aunt said, "but mind the back of her dress does not get soiled, and be aware that although it may appear we are out in the middle of nowhere, we *do* get a goodly amount of traffic on the main road. Who can tell whether someone may glance towards the house while on their travels and *spot* you both?"

The old woman's implication shocked me to the core, though why it did, and why I thought she should not voice such concerns, I did not know. I should have been grateful she cared about Pearl and her reputation—or was it her own? I admitted in that moment that our marriage could not come soon enough. Pearl would fare better away from this sour lady.

But we have yet to discuss what will happen in the future. Everything was pushed aside for...other things.

Determined to make solid plans, I nodded to Mistress Lewis even though she did not see the gesture, then crooked my arm. Pearl walked to my side and slid her hand into the space. We left together, without speaking until we reached the relative seclusion at the side of the house.

Pearl launched herself at me, winding her hands around my neck and fingering my hair. She kissed me, long and deep, and I found myself responding with more ardour than I should have, given our location.

Reluctantly, I pulled away. "Much as I am relieved that you still want me, we cannot do this here. Your aunt may well be watching." I glanced behind at windows the old lady could be standing behind. Returning my gaze to Pearl, I could not stop a smile spreading. She was so delightful, so unlike any other woman, that my heart clenched with love for her. "I am so terribly sorry she knows of my nocturnal visits."

Pearl set her jaw and lifted her chin. "I do not care. She has never wanted me in her life. I am nothing but a burden. News of our marriage was secretly very welcome, I am sure. I do not think it would even matter if I was against it. She would have accepted your offer just as quickly, to be rid of me."

I stroked a strand of hair back from her face. "I do not understand her. If she is so convinced I am a bad man, why allow you to marry me?"

"I have never understood her and never will."

"I see. What do you wish for her once we are married? That she live at my home with us?"

For a fleeting second, indecision flickered over Pearl's features, then she said, "No. I will sound selfish, but I do not wish to live with her a moment longer than I have to. She is unwell, I know that, but perhaps we could employ a nurse who will see to her needs. She could have my larger bedroom when I vacate."

Once again, Pearl wanted what I did, yet knowing Pearl's aunt was a less than kindly woman, I worried that Pearl's abandonment of her would reflect badly on my soon-to-be wife. "People may find that arrangement odd."

"They may, but I can assure you, Aunt Edith will not want to leave here." She toyed with the hair at my temple.

I resisted the urge to kiss her again, instead putting space between us. "Then we must at least offer that I come and live in this house. If she refuses, then we have nothing to feel badly for."

"Indeed. Oh, James, I just want...us. Alone."

With her use of my middle name, the past suddenly loomed behind me like a tangible shadow, lending weight to my shoulders. "Are you sure? We have much to talk about. What if you change your mind? The rosy hue of this wonderful time may well be clouding your judgement."

She frowned, hurt showing on her features. "Are you trying to tell me something?"

I tugged her towards me, crushing her to my chest and holding her head to my shoulder. She wore no coat—our rush to be out of that room had seen to that—and I worried she might be cold. "God, no. I just want you to be sure. The changing of minds happens, Pearl. Everything will be fine. I will look after you, keep you safe for the rest of your life. I promise."

She reared back to look at me. Her eyes filled with tears and one spilled over, coursing down her cheek. I wiped it away with a thumb, my chest constricting with emotion. I wished we were already married, that I could tuck her into my carriage and take her home, making love to her for hours until she could take no more. My body responded to hers being so close, and my cock hardened. She smiled as she felt me burgeon and eyed me with the lust in her eyes I had come to love.

Tugging me towards the back of the house, she said, "There is a secret place here we can visit. No one will see us from the house."

"But we must return inside. You have no coat. It is too cold out here."

She ignored me, so I sighed and followed, trying to slow her pace so we did not appear to be rushing. But, God, I wanted to rush. Her proximity drove me insane, and I needed a hefty dose of her. She led me through a thick stand of trees and bushes, bringing me to a clearing.

A small pond with large lilies sat in the centre, reminding me that she had so recently used Lily as a name. The grass beside the pond was long, a haven for insects, damp from the still-lingering fog. The chill in the air gave me pause. I could not undress her here.

Pearl hugged my arm and stood on tiptoe to kiss my cheek. "Take me here."

I smiled at her obvious need and glanced around. "It is wet. You will get cold. You must already *be* cold."

"Not if you just lift my skirts. And you could warm me up."

She smiled so sweetly I would swear she had not just uttered those words.

Her desire transferred to me, and I looked about with a coupling in mind. I envisaged how I could give my lady what she wanted without soiling her dress.

"Come here." I pulled her to me. "This will be a lesson in you doing most of the work."

Pearl stood before me and gathered her skirts to her waist. I stared at her long, slender legs and up to the juncture between. She wore no under garments. My God, that woman never ceased to amaze me. She had planned it all along, the vixen. I freed my cock and gripped her sides, hoisting her up so her hot, wet cunt warmed my lower belly. She draped her arms over my shoulders and laced her chilled hands behind my neck. My length nudged the cleft of her backside, the heat of flesh on flesh making me throb.

"Woman, you are truly a rarity."

She leaned her torso away, hanging her head back, and a giddy laugh floated from her lips. The column of her neck invited me to lick it, but our position prevented such a luxury. Pearl straightened and appraised me with such intensity that my heart skipped a beat. Unable to resist her, I lifted her by the waist and settled my cock tip at her opening. She pushed down, her sheath clamping around me, and I worried that I would hurt her again.

"Take it slow," I cautioned, her juices soaking my cock. "You are not used to this. It may still hurt."

146

"It feels wonderful this time," she said, smiling again. "Help me to please you."

As she held firm about my neck, Pearl eased herself up and down, aided by my hands on her waist. Her tightness... it was almost too much.

I kissed her neck, saying between pecks, "Cross your ankles."

She obeyed, her inner thighs pressing close, and I widened my legs for better balance and purchase on the ground. She upped her pace, caressing the side of my head with her cheek, and I lowered my mouth to her chest, forgetting her dress covered the swells I sought to suckle.

"Show me your breasts," I whispered, watching as she took one hand from my neck and fumbled to unbutton the front of her dress. Her slim fingers did something to me, spurring images of Pearl touching her private space between her legs. I wanted to watch her do that and vowed to ask her to show me how she enjoyed being touched. "God, you are gorgeous."

Pearl continued to rise and fall, taking me very close to an edge I did not want to fall over just then. She scooped one breast from her dress, then the other, the generous globes a sight to behold—firm, with taut peaks and rosy circles around them. The cold had made her nipples stand up higher than they usually would, and my cock throbbed in response at seeing them. She placed her hand back around my neck, and I lost no time in sucking one nipple into my mouth and swirling my tongue over it. Her gasp of pleasure set my cock to throbbing harder. I concentrated on keeping a firm footing but failed, staggering back a step or two.

"Let me kneel," I said.

With reluctance, I set her on the ground. Her dress swished down to cover her legs, and I could not wait for her to reveal them again. Kneeling, uncaring that the grass would sully my clothing, I took her hand and tugged her down so she knelt too, bringing her sheath back on to my cock.

I moved one hand from her waist and snaked it between us, reaching down to her folds. While tending to her nipple, I rubbed her bud, my circular, slick movements aided by her abundance of cream. The sweet smell of her drifted up, filling my nose and making me want to place her on the ground and thrust inside her at my own pace. Pearl planted her feet on the grass, using the leverage to piston up and down, harder, faster, tighter.

I released her nipple and looked at her face, with those closed eyes and flushed cheeks. She appeared serene, at peace with our joining, and I marvelled that such a woman wanted to be with me. How lucky I was to have her.

The beat in my cock intensified, and my bollocks tautened. Pearl's body stiffened, then she arched her back, her nub pushing against my fingers. Channel clenching, she let out a ragged gasp, and her pelvis bucked as she maintained her rhythm. Her pleasure had begun to hit, and I applied more pressure, rubbing faster and jamming her down on to me, fingers digging into her waist. I dipped my head, sucking on her nipple, and she cried out, scraping her nails down my neck. My own bliss spiralled through me a second before I ejaculated, the force of the jet speeding out so fast I lost my breath. Pearl gasped, and her inner walls squeezed me, aiding the rest of my seed's exit. We were both spent, and I slowed my fingers as she slowed her movement. She stopped and looked down at me, and I raised my hand from her folds and sucked my fingers.

Eyes wide, she said, "I have, without a doubt, fallen in love with you."

Those words, branded into my mind and heart, will remain with me forever.

Chapter Twelve

November 11th, 1888

Pearl stood on the step outside her front door and raised a hand in goodbye. She did not want James to leave, but the grass stains on his knees gave away their activities. Her aunt had good eyesight—as well as restored hearing, it seemed—and Pearl could not suffer any more degradation from her today.

James would be back soon, for dinner, and she reminded herself to let Annabel know that she may be requested to stay the night. His carriage reached the end of the driveway, and Pearl waited until it had disappeared along the main road before going back inside the house. She smelt of him, still felt his hands on her, and his seed seeped between her legs.

I never want to wash him away.

She wandered into the drawing room, hoping her aunt had retired to her room. She had not. The old woman still sat on the window seat, looking out the glass. Her rigid back and straightened shoulders shouted her anger. Taking a deep breath to prepare herself for the verbal assault she sensed coming, Pearl sat in her usual chair and picked up her sewing for something to occupy her hands. Her aunt did not speak, and the air held a chill, as though the venom inside the woman had bled out. Pearl remained silent, bending her head to her task, and awaited the vitriol.

It started with a sigh, jagged and broken, then a swish of fabric as Edith stood from the seat and walked to stand in front of the fireplace. Pearl disguised a sigh of her own, trying hard to still her now shaking hands.

"I expected more from you, Pearl."

Ah, so that was the road her aunt was going to take.

"Did you throw yourself at him? Did you realise that your ideals were too high, that you would be left on the shelf in the not too distant future, stooping so low as to choose a man who had a hand in killing my brother?"

"James did not—" Pearl stopped herself. If she defended James, let her aunt know how much she wanted to marry him, the old woman might change her mind and refuse to give her blessing.

"His name is not James but Seth. Another deception on his part. What a grand way to start your relationship. With lies and deceit."

"I am aware of what his name is. I prefer to call him James," Pearl lied. She would always think of him as James and call him such. After all, she had met him as James, and the name suited him. "So we have not started anything with lies and deceit. The only lies and deceit have come from you telling me he had a hand in my father's death when he did not, and it has made me wonder what other untruths you have told me." She swallowed, then took a deep breath. "I do not know what I have done to deserve such treatment from you. You have never liked me, but I do know that leaving you here alone will not bother me in the slightest now. You have made it quite clear how you feel. Therefore, you will not want to live with us once we are married."

She flounced out of the room before her aunt could retaliate, and rushed to her bedroom. It smelt of James, of her cream, and she flopped on to the bed, inhaling deeply as though the aromas could console her.

They did somewhat, and she rested for a while, contemplating James's visit at dinnertime and dreaming how the rest of their lives would be. Around an hour later, Annabel's timid knock sounded on the door, and Pearl rose from the bed to sit on the edge.

"Come in," she said, watching the maid scuttle in, a newspaper in her hand.

"Your aunt suggested that I bring up the newspaper and ask if you would like some tea, miss."

Pearl widened her eyes then disguised her reaction. Perhaps her sharp words to the old woman had hit home. "Oh, thank you, Annabel."

The maid handed Pearl the newspaper. "And your aunt said a messenger boy brought word that Frances would be calling presently."

Frances? Whatever could she want? She had never called unless they had arranged it.

"Did the boy say if anything was wrong?"

"I don't know, miss. Your aunt don't tell me nothing like that." She smiled, then asked, "Would you like some tea brought up, miss?"

"Yes, please, Annabel." Pearl placed the newspaper beside her on the bed. "Oh, and would you mind staying the night again? Mr Adams will be coming to dinner."

"I don't mind, miss. Better than going home." She bobbed then moved backward to the door. "Would you mind if I say something out of turn, miss?" Annabel looked worried. She wrung her hands and bit her bottom lip.

"I do not mind in the slightest. It is my aunt who minds. Do go ahead."

"I couldn't help but overhear, miss, that you're getting married. If you don't mind, may I come with you? I don't want to be left here with…with her, miss."

Annabel's blush tugged at Pearl's heart. She had not given the maid a second thought, being so caught up in her own affairs. Guilt bloomed inside her. How could she have forgotten the loyal little maid?

"Of course you may come with me, although I daresay Mr Adams has his own staff. I do not doubt for one minute that you will not be allowed to come. Let us say you are my personal maid, yes? Would that suit?"

The maid moved to dart forward, perhaps to fling herself

into Pearl's arms, but she remembered her place and remained where she was. Pearl stood and held out her arms, once again shunning propriety by offering the young woman a warm embrace. Annabel felt frail against her, as though she had not eaten much lately, and Pearl vowed to speak to her more thoroughly to find out whether her job here included food.

For now, she said, "And a piece of cake would not go amiss, am I correct?" Pearl released the young woman and held her at arm's length. "If you would please bring a large slice up here with my tea, I should like you to remain in here and eat it."

Annabel widened her eyes. "Oh, no, miss. That wouldn't be allowed. Your aunt—"

"Will not have to be told. Now go. Cake and tea, yes? If you can manage to bring two cups up here without her seeing, I should like you to join me for a few minutes. After all, we have your future position to discuss, do we not?"

The maid's eyes filled with tears. "Yes, miss. We do, miss. Thank you."

She dashed out of the room, her heavy boots loud on the wooden landing floor. Pearl swallowed a lump in her throat and chastised herself for being so blind as to what had been in front of her all along.

She wondered where Annabel lived. In Whitechapel? Pearl shuddered and her guilt grew. Perhaps, if James would allow it, the young woman could live with them permanently.

While Pearl waited for her maid to return, she read the front page of the newspaper. More shocking revelations on Mary Kelly's murder. Whoever was committing these atrocious acts would surely be caught. He could not continue in this vein indefinitely. She shuddered as an image of the man at the club came to mind, and to ward off any further thoughts of him, she opened the paper to browse other news.

A man had been found dead in the early hours, it seemed,

on the roadside not far from this very house. The reporter speculated as to what he was doing out and about during the night in such an out-of-the-way place. The city proper was not too far away, but the road in question gave rise to musings on whether he had been forced there in his carriage and killed or waylaid by another driver.

Thinking no more of it, Pearl closed the paper, folded it, and stood, placing it on the small occasional table beside the door. Annabel knocked, then entered, bearing a tray with a huge slab of fruit cake and the necessaries for drinking tea. Pearl was pleased to see two cups on the tray and beckoned Annabel to sit on the bed while she poured the steaming brew. Finished, she sat beside the maid, relieved her of the tray, and urged her to eat the cake.

While Annabel ate, Pearl mused aloud on what the maid's duties would be once she left this damnable house. She got quite carried away, imagining her future life, and possibly said a little more than she should have. However, she told herself that if Annabel was to be her personal maid, it would do no harm to get her used to such private ramblings. Better to find out whether Annabel gossiped sooner rather than later, but she trusted her instincts. This young woman would suit her nicely.

Pearl trailed off, and the companionable silence between them gave her a chance to think on why Frances felt the need to visit again so soon after her last call. She dreaded her visit in case something was wrong and selfishly did not want to have anything spoiling her newfound happiness. Was it evil to feel this way? To have had her share of unhappiness and now want to keep hold of what she had found and cherish it?

"What time will Frances be arriving?" she asked Annabel, who scooped up the last of the cake crumbs and paused before popping them into her mouth.

She swallowed, then said, "In about half an hour, miss."

Pearl nodded. "And where is Aunt Edith?"

"She's taking a nap, miss."

Pearl smiled conspiratorially. "Then I suggest you take this opportunity to return the tray to the kitchen, wash the cups, and put them away."

Annabel stood and collected the tray. She hesitated at the door, her back presented to Pearl. "Thank you, miss. For everything you said. I won't let you down."

She left the room, this time on quieter feet, and Annabel smiled, smoothing her bed covers for something to do before Frances arrived. Anxiety gnawed at her gut, and she could not shake the feeling that her world was about to be turned upside down. After walking several laps of her room, she made her way downstairs, entering the drawing room to find the fire out and a distinct chill in the air. It added to the foreboding already inside her, and rather than distract Annabel from her task of concealing the evidence that she had taken tea and eaten cake, Pearl set about starting the fire again herself.

She heard the crunch of gravel outside. She went to the window and peered out. Frances alighted from her carriage, her face pinched and drawn, and walked up the front steps. She looked ill.

Pearl rushed to the front door and flung it wide, staring at Frances as her friend walked in. "What has happened? Are you all right?"

Frances glanced about the foyer, then up at the stairway. "Are you alone?" she whispered, tilting her head towards the drawing room.

"Yes. My aunt is taking a nap."

"Good."

Frances divested herself of her light blue coat, and Pearl took it from her, hanging it in a closet beside the stairs. Tense, Pearl led the way into the drawing room, gesturing for Frances to sit. She rang the bell for Annabel and waited in the doorway, instructing the maid to bring tea quickly. Closing the door, she rested her back against it and took in Frances's appearance. She wore a drab grey dress, similar to the type Annabel wore, the fabric of better quality but the style doing nothing for Frances's attributes. Whatever had happened must have shocked her friend, for she looked as though she was quite out of sorts.

Pearl walked across the room and sat in the chair she always used, the small table between hers and Frances's. "What the devil has happened?"

What if she has been found out for leaving the house the other night?

Frances cast a nervous glance at the door and opened her mouth to speak. She did not manage to utter a word before Annabel knocked and came in with the tea trolley. Frustrated at the interruption but unable to say anything, for she had ordered the tea and caused the intrusion, Pearl nodded to Annabel.

After the maid left, Pearl poured Frances a cup, hoping the sweetness of the brew would go some way to helping her with whatever shock she had endured.

Frances sipped then placed her cup back on the trolley. She looked at Pearl. "Luke is dead."

Pearl's stomach contracted. "Pardon? Luke the carriage driver?"

"Yes." The word came out as a whisper, and Frances lifted one hand to cover her mouth. Her eyes moistened. "He did not return to the house after...after that night. I thought...my parents thought he had taken his usual day off, but when he still did not come back..."

"Oh my goodness. What happened?" Pearl laid a palm over her heart. It beat too hard and too fast, and her head lightened.

"Our carriage was found abandoned on the outskirts of town, not a scratch on it. Luke lay beside it."

"Dear God. He had an accident, then. Perhaps he left the club for a ride, thinking to return and collect us later?"

"No. He had been killed."

The room spun. Pearl gasped sharply, her mind awhirl with the horror of what her friend had imparted. "Killed? What? How?"

"It seems he may have been coerced into offering someone a ride. Maybe someone from the club."

Frances eyed her meaningfully, but Pearl could not grasp what the look meant. Shock had rendered her speechless, and her stomach felt as though it had hollowed. Was Luke the man reported in the newspaper?

"I have my suspicions about who it was," Frances continued, turning to stare out the window.

Pearl followed her gaze and saw the coach still there, the driver clapping his hands, undoubtedly for warmth. "Would your new driver... Would he like to come in? He could have tea in the kitchen with Annabel."

Frances shook her head. "I cannot stay long. I have time to drink my tea then I must return home. My parents are distraught. They have known Luke since he was a small boy." She smiled wistfully. "As have I." With a sigh, she said, "I shall confess now that our jaunt to the club...my saying I did not want to be married yet... It was all a lie. I had wanted to force Luke's hand. I wanted him to ask me to marry him. It would not have been a good match in society's eyes, but I loved him dearly, and..." A sob caught in her throat.

Pearl dashed from her seat to kneel at Frances's feet. "Oh, my love. I am so terribly sorry for your loss." She thought of how she would feel if it were James taken from her so despicably, and tears burned her eyes. "I had no idea you felt this way about Luke." She took Frances's hands in hers and brushed her thumbs over the cold skin.

"I...I did not think you would approve." Frances stared at Pearl, her eyes swimming in tears, her cheeks red and blotchy. "But I should have known you better."

Pearl silently admitted the truth of Frances's statement, but now was not the time to dwell on the pinch of hurt. She had to push her feelings aside. "My dearest friend, I will always support you. Whatever you wish to tell me will remain with me, and I will help you with any future decisions you make. It is not about loving someone other people approve of, I know that now, but someone you can see yourself happy with."

Frances nodded. "Luke was the only one…" She gave a forced, tight smile and abruptly rose. "I have to go. I shall focus on getting my parents through this time. Perhaps that will save me from wallowing in my own grief."

Pearl stood and embraced Frances, the woman's body feeling frail like Annabel's had. "But you must take the time to grieve for yourself. I do not want you becoming ill."

Frances pulled away and walked to the door. She turned with her hand on the knob and gave a wan smile. "I will never be the same again. It was my silly plan to go to the club. My fault Luke was killed. I will never forgive myself."

Pearl's heart constricted with pity. She would feel the same way if it had been her.

After collecting Frances's coat and sending her friend home with the knowledge she would be available if needed, Pearl returned to the drawing room. This turn of events was so awful that she took a moment to sit on the window seat and digest it.

Luke had been lured away from the club. Possibly by someone from the club? Who had Frances meant? Pearl's stomach plummeted. Surely she had not implied James had done this?

No. No, that is not possible.

Who then?

She pondered things for a long time until, unable to sit a moment longer, she left the room and took a thick shawl from the closet. Out on the front step, she glanced around, wary as the memory of the death reported in the paper came to mind. Someone was out there not only killing women but men too. She would not walk along the main road as she sometimes did to clear her mind. No, she would remain on the grounds. It was safer that way.

She strolled the path she had taken earlier with James, intent on visiting the secret place where they had made love. How a few hours changed one's life! Last time she had been here she'd been happy, and now she was consumed with grief on her friend's behalf. She could discuss it with James when he arrived for dinner and find the best way to console Frances without smothering her too much.

Beside the pond, she stared at the water, darkened to black by the onset of night. The moon hid behind the clouds, giving scant illumination on the water's surface, but enough light that Pearl could see the lilies floating.

Lily. It seemed so long ago that she had been that person, yet it had been such a short time. A faint smile touched her lips as she thought of the many nights ahead where she could become Lily again. Her life had taken a wonderful turn, yet her friend's had not. The intrusion of Frances in her mind again made Pearl consider who had enticed Luke from his post—it would have been a clever person to convince the young man to disobey orders to remain in place. She shuddered and tightened the shawl around her, aghast that such despicable people existed, and racked her mind to figure out who it could be.

A twig snapping behind her brought a rash of goose-bumps to her skin, and her heart hammered, pulse thudding in her ears. She spun around, instinct screaming at her that danger lurked nearby. Gaze darting every which way, she eyed her surroundings, finding no one. She stared through the opening of the secret place and to the house, the darkened grounds, and dashed forward to make her way to the safety of her home. At the opening, a hand shot out from the trees and clamped about her neck, cutting off any chance she had of screaming. She was yanked backward against what was undoubtedly a man's chest, and hot, sour-smelling breath warmed her cheek.

Frantic, she flailed her hands and lifted one foot to jab backward at her assailant's legs, only to find her foot met nothing but air. Her lungs burned—God, how she needed air—and in a last ditch attempt to free herself, she raised her arms and grabbed at the man's head, her fingers coming into contact with a hat.

Oh, God. Please do not let me die. Not now. Not when I have found James…

She struggled, bucking and writhing for freedom. With a suddenness that startled her, the hand left her neck and gripped her upper arm. She sucked in a blessed lungful of air. Her throat ached, was so sore, and her attempted scream came out as nothing more than a hoarse croak. Whoever stood behind her wrenched her to face him, and she stared up into the face of a man she had seen all too recently.

The man from the club leered down at her, the whites of his eyes and his teeth obscenely bright considering the darkness.

"Now, then," he said on an exhale. "Let's be nice and quiet while we find somewhere to get better acquainted."

"What do you want?" she managed, hoping to gain some time to think on how to get away from him.

"I want…" He smiled. "You."

Chapter Thirteen

November 11th, 1888

The Dairy of Seth Adams

After putting word about that I had been courting Pearl and that we would be married within a month, I readied myself for our upcoming dinner. I decided to leave early, intent on snatching some time alone with her before Annabel's interruptions during the meal. We had much to discuss, and I could not wait to be in her company again. I hired a hansom and left earlier than planned. On the ride to her home, I mulled over the events I had gleaned from the newspaper. It seemed Percival Sloker had been found, and by God I should not have been pleased that he was dead, but I was. That I had a hand in his demise gave only a niggle of remorse, and I told myself I had rid London of a man who had committed several murders. I had saved lives.

Without dwelling on him further, I arrived at Pearl's and sent the cab driver away. Taking a deep breath, I knocked on the front door, hoping my beautiful lady would be the one to open it. She was not. Annabel stood before me, her eyes alight with hope that had not been present before, and I wondered what had given the young woman cause to appear so happy.

"Good evening, sir." She curtseyed and allowed me entrance. "I'll fetch Miss Pearl. If I could take your coat?"

I handed it to her, watched her thin form as she scuttled to the closet and secreted my garment inside. She dashed up the stairs and disappeared in the gloom of the unlit landing. I laced my fingers and rocked on my feet, gaze fixed up there so I did not miss sight of Pearl emerging from her room. My hopes were dashed with the re-emergence of Annabel, looking worried as she clutched the banister rail and leant forward.

"Miss Pearl isn't in her room, sir. I'll just check to see whether she's in with her aunt."

I nodded and smiled, then took it upon myself to look in the drawing room. She was not there, so I peeked inside the other rooms on the ground floor. As I returned to the foyer, Annabel and Pearl's aunt were coming down the stairs. The maid's face was drawn, and she wrung her hands. The aunt, however, stared at me with a hint of scorn and lifted her haughty chin as she approached and stood before me.

"I am not a stupid woman, Seth Adams," she said, glaring at me with eyes as grey as her hair. "Do you think I am not aware that you are trying to fool me into thinking you were not in the back copse just moments ago with Pearl?"

I frowned. "I most certainly was not, madam. I have only just arrived by hansom." My heart beat faster. "Are you saying Pearl is outside in the *dark?*"

Good God. Whatever was the woman thinking, letting her go outside when night drew near?

"Oh, Mr Adams. You are very good. Perhaps you should have taken to the stage instead of running a brewery."

The old woman's sneer stuck in my craw, and I held back from gripping her scrawny arm and shaking her.

"I assure you I am not lying. I have not seen Pearl since I was here earlier." I walked away from her, throwing over my shoulder, "And if she is outside now, I would rather be out there myself to ensure she comes back inside than arguing in here with you."

Incensed, I stormed out and rounded the side of the house, stalking towards our secret place as though the devil were on my tail. What had Pearl been thinking, taking a walk in the dark without Annabel or even her surly little aunt?

I walked through the bushes into the clearing and glanced around, expecting to see her beside the pond or pacing the grass. She was not there, and the first real sense of alarm hit me. I searched the surrounding trees, peering through the trunks and studying the ground at their bases. It had not been disturbed, and neither had the grass except for where we had coupled earlier.

Anger and fear grew, and I strode towards the opening, my gaze drawn to a patch of grass that was well-trodden, with churned earth that indicated someone had stood there very recently. Had she made those divots?

Back at the house, I sought out Annabel, finding her in the kitchen with one hand to her chin. She gnawed her lower lip, and I was gratified someone else cared for Pearl enough to be worried by her absence.

She whipped her head to face me as I entered, her eyes wide and full of worry. "Was she out there, sir?"

"No, she was not. Do you know why on earth she may have gone outside alone?" I came abreast of her and placed my hand on her arm to give her some comfort. "What did she do after I left earlier?"

Annabel pulled a handkerchief from her sleeve and dabbed her eyes. "We took tea and cake together, sir," she whispered, gaze darting to the kitchen door. "At her insistence. She offered for me to come and live with you as her personal maid. Then Miss Frances came. I made them tea, and when I went back to collect the trolley the drawing room was empty. I thought...I thought Miss Pearl had gone to her room after Miss Frances had left, sir." She widened her eyes. "I should have checked. I should have made sure. I—"

"It is all right. It is more important that we find her now. Did you check every room upstairs?"

"Not yet, sir. Her aunt...she said Pearl was outside. Called her a whore, she did..."

The old woman's words burned in my gut, and I clamped my jaw before saying, "Then go and check the rooms now and anywhere else in the house you think she might be. I will go back outside. Is there anywhere she could be on the grounds other than the copse? Anywhere she likes to go?"

"She usually just walks, sir. But there's a little cottage behind the copse. Used to belong to the gardener years ago when we had one. Might she have gone there?"

I took no time to answer. The fire in my belly to find my lady spurred me back outside, and I ran to the copse and through the trees. The thick leaves of the pines stole the poor excuse of moonlight, and I staggered several times on the uneven ground before catching sight of an opening ahead. Pushing myself harder, breaths coming out hard and fast, I ploughed through the tree line and out the other side.

A faint light flickered beyond a small, dirty window in a weather-beaten cottage, and relief poured through me. She was here, had perhaps come for a bit of peace and solitude.

Without slowing my pace, I reached the small wooden gate separating the grounds from a tiny front garden, my attention drawn to the window. She *was* inside, as I saw a figure walk in front of a lighted candle on what appeared to be a wooden sideboard. I stepped through the over-long grass to watch her for a moment, to take a secret minute to observe her beauty without her knowledge. The pane of glass was indeed dirty, but not so much that I could not see inside. Pearl sat on a blue settee, a swathe of candlelight to the right illuminating one side of her face. It seemed she stared at the bare wooden flooring without seeing anything at all, and her expression, one of intense thought, brought a different fear to my gut. Was she having second thoughts?

I leaned closer, squinted harder and frowned at her hands clasped in her lap.

Her wrists appeared to be bound by coarse rope.

I sucked in a breath, momentarily stunned into inaction. My attention was drawn to a fleeting wisp of movement in the far left corner, and the sight of a shadowed, smiling face looking at Pearl prompted me to act. I could not see who it was, but it was a man. I had no idea why she would be here with a fellow and did not care to hang around outside long enough to find out. That she was bound and with another man was enough to have me leaving that window and reaching for the front door knob.

What if Pearl is here with him because she chose it? Because she wanted to be Lily with someone else?

I dashed that thought away, furious with myself for even entertaining such an idea. I trusted Pearl. There was no way on this earth she was here of her own free will. I turned the handle, glad it offered no resistance. Opening the door quietly and stepping inside, I kept to the far left of a small hallway to enable to me pass the door to the room on the right where Pearl and the man were. I crossed to the doorway and pressed myself against the wall. I considered bursting in and knocking the man senseless, but I wanted to get a measure of what this was about before I did such a thing.

My earlier thought nagged again. *She may be here to be Lily.* I hated myself for it.

Pearl sniffled, and my senses went into overdrive. She did not have a cold, should not be sniffling unless she was upset. I fought the urge to rush in and grab her, to confront the bastard.

"He will be here shortly," the man said. "And before he arrives, I must do to you what I have done to other whores just like you."

My stomach muscles clenched as I recognised the voice. Dear God, she was in the room with Percival Sloker. How could that be? He was dead, damn it!

I eased my head around so I could look into the room. A floorboard creaked slightly with my movement, and Pearl slowly lifted her gaze from the floor to glance at me. She did not show delight at my being there, merely blinked as though she had not seen me and turned her gaze to the corner where I had seen Sloker's shadow through the window.

"You will not get away with this," she said, her red hair burnished to copper by the candlelight. "I do not understand what you hope to achieve, and I do not for one minute believe that James left you on the road like you said."

The sight of Sloker coming out of his corner to block my view of Pearl tested my endurance to stay put.

"He left me there for dead, make no mistake about that. He knows who I am, and I cannot have him walking around with such knowledge. Once I am done with you, I will also deal with him." He laughed gently. "And will look forward to reading the newspaper tomorrow."

I had a clear chance to rush forward and grab hold of him, but at the moment the thought entered my mind, I noticed he held a long-bladed knife by his side. If I caught hold of him wrong, if we toppled off balance... I could not risk Pearl coming to any harm. With care, I reached inside my coat and curled my fingers around the small pistol I had placed there since fighting with Sloker before. I would not shoot to kill — the bullet might go through him to Pearl — but aim for his calf instead.

Bringing the pistol out, I lifted my arm to take aim. A brief movement through the glass panes in the front door snatched my attention, and as I turned my head to quickly glance at what it was, the front door burst open. I returned to my hidden spot beside the door, hoping Sloker would think it was I who had arrived.

Pearl's aunt barrelled towards me, fists on her hips. "I thought I might find you here. I had a feeling this would be your secret place for a tryst."

She had said too much, so the widening of my eyes in an attempt to make her close her mouth was wasted. So intent was she in her rant, she possibly failed to notice my warning and continued on, standing on the other side of the door.

"Where are you, Pearl?" the old woman demanded, her reedy voice shriller than I thought possible.

What was going on in that room? Had Sloker seized Pearl

and held the knife to her throat? Pearl's whimper and a scuffle told me that was a high possibility, and I clenched my teeth and glared at her aunt. Pearl's mewl brought the aunt to the doorway, and I hoped Sloker would think she had been shouting at Pearl when she had burst in and not at me.

"Oh my goodness! What are you doing with my niece? Unhand her at once!"

I stared at Pearl's aunt, amazed that she did not bat an eyelid at the scene before her. My guts churned as I thought of where Percival's hands were.

"And using a knife on a woman? Really! Do you not have any decorum?"

Anger boiled inside me. The aunt stormed into the room, and I peeked as much as I dared around the doorframe, hoping to God Sloker would not see me. I wanted the element of surprise.

He stood facing the doorway, Pearl held with her back to his chest. The knife was not at her throat as I had envisaged, but hovering over her heart. A quick flash of how the other women had been killed came, and I swallowed to combat my rising nausea. I could not allow him to pierce Pearl's skin with that blade, to gut her as though she was nothing more than an animal to be butchered.

The old woman stopped in front of him, hands jammed to her waist. "Put that knife down this instant and let my niece go."

A sly smile spread on Sloker's face, and I knew instinctually that he was about to do something the old woman would regret. With Pearl's safety uppermost in my mind, I had no choice but to join the tableau. I stepped into the room, praying to God I had done the right thing, and aimed the gun at Sloker. His gaze slid from the old woman to me, and I stared at him hard, wanting to get across to him that he had better not try anything stupid.

As though I meant nothing to him, that I was of no threat or consequence whatsoever, he looked at the old woman again. "Whores do not belong. And this young woman is a whore."

"Let her go," I said, taking another step forward. "She is not what you think."

"Then why was she at the club?" Percival kept his gaze on the aunt.

"Club?" she asked. "What club?"

I took a second to look at Pearl. Tears fell down her flushed cheeks, and she stared at me as though this was the last time she would ever see me. I would not let that be so. We were to spend the rest of our lives together, and no one would stand in the way of that.

"A whore's club," Percival said. "Your niece works in one. Plies her trade. Is used in base ways by men willing to pay her for the pleasure."

The old woman laughed. "Oh, you speak such nonsense. You have her confused with someone else."

Sloker narrowed his eyes, as though a delicious thought had come to mind. "Whore's aunts should be punished too."

He lunged forward, sinking the blade into the old woman's belly, Pearl stuck between them. At the same moment she shrieked and struggled to get out of Sloker's hold, I dove forward and covered his face with my palm in an attempt to shove him backward. He remained rigid in his position, an immovable mountain. I pushed again, looking over my shoulder at the old woman.

Sloker jerked his arm, and Pearl pulled away from him, standing beside her aunt to watch in stunned horror as the blade, still embedded, slid upward. Blood oozed out of the old woman's mouth, and her eyes, wide with shock, stared straight ahead at her attacker. Pearl's scream wrenched at my heart, and I swiftly brought up my gun arm and fired a bullet into Sloker's face. He reeled backward, hand coming free of the knife handle, his head smacking the mantel behind him as Pearl's aunt slumped to the floor.

Ignoring Sloker, for I had no doubt he was dead, I turned

my attention to the figure on the floor and that of my kneeling love beside it. Pearl sobbed, trying to staunch the copious flow of blood from the gaping wound in her aunt's stomach as best she could with her bound hands. I kneeled at the old woman's other side and checked whether she breathed. She did not.

Looking up, I caught Pearl's eye and tried to convey my sorrow that her aunt had gone. From Pearl's distraught expression, I knew the words she had spoken earlier about disliking the old woman had been said in anger.

"My love," I said, extending a hand to lie upon her arm. "We must report this to the authorities immediately."

She nodded and swallowed a hiccoughing sob. "I...I did love her really."

"I know, love. I know."

Chapter Fourteen

November 12th, 1888

Pearl woke, though she did not open her eyes. For a second she studied the orange glow of her closed eyelids and knew the sun shone through her bedroom window despite the winter day. The terrible events came back to her in a rush of images, and she snapped her eyes open to make them go away. Her heart rate sped, and she coached herself to remain calm. That man was not coming back, could not harm her now, yet his touch seemed branded on her skin. His scent remained despite her bathing before bed, and his voice lingered in her mind, his caustic words echoing.

How long would it be before the memories faded? They were as bright now as they had been last night, and she longed for the day the grief subsided. Surely there would be a day when she could remember this time in her life without shuddering?

She swung her legs out of bed and sat up, staring out the window at the blue sky. It gave a false illusion of everything being all right, that if the sun shone then nothing could taint the day. How wrong that was. Sighing, she got out of bed and went to the window, the air chilly on her face and neck.

There was no point in lighting a fire, for she did not intend staying in her room for much longer. She had another visit from the authorities this afternoon. They wanted to check her version of events one more time before they closed the case.

With no energy to put on her robe, she closed her eyes and thought of the copse, the cottage. A shiver rippled up her spine and lifted the hairs at her nape. She would be glad to be away from this place, to sell it and never return. It held too many sorrows now.

Her aunt's body had been taken away, as had that dreaded man's. She considered her feelings about the old woman. Although Aunt Edith had been surly and had given the impression she had not cared one jot for Pearl, her courage in confronting Percival Sloker had proved otherwise. Why had she been so abrasive, so abrupt with Pearl, when she had cared deep down?

Why had I been the same way towards her?

Perhaps she had not wanted to show Pearl affection through fear of losing her as she had lost her brother. Her aunt had been different when Pearl was a child, friendlier, a woman who smiled a little more and did not inspire feelings of unease. It had only been as she grew that Pearl had noticed changes in the older woman. Maybe she had been scorned in love. Maybe that was why she had agreed to James's proposal of marriage—she would rather Pearl loved someone than no one at all. But Pearl had not tried to get to know the woman better, to understand her, and now it was too late.

Instead of allowing these thoughts to manifest into a huge ball of pain, she switched them off and prepared to get washed and dressed. As she filled the china bowl on her sideboard and dipped in a washcloth, a soft knock came at her door.

"Come in," she said, throat sore, her voice hoarse.

Annabel walked in, bearing a tray of tea and toast. "I thought you might be hungry, miss."

"Thank you, Annabel. How are you this morning?"

The poor girl had taken a funny turn when Pearl and James had returned to the house, their clothes and hands bloodstained. She had fainted, and Pearl had brought her around with smelling salts, putting her to bed after a brief explanation.

"I'm all right, thank you, miss. Still a bit shocked, but I'll be fine." She tried to smile brightly and added, "Mr Adams is downstairs."

Pearl's heart fluttered. "He is? It may be improper to do so, but this morning I do not care. Would you send him up?"

Annabel nodded.

"And please make sure to eat breakfast yourself. We should get a visit from the authorities again today, and after that we have a funeral and wedding to prepare for. We will be busy, so you must eat to keep up your strength."

"As you say, miss."

Annabel left the room. Pearl washed hurriedly, the scent of lavender soap masking the residual odour of Percival Sloker. But she was sure he still remained. Would that smell ever disappear? She blinked away the image of him leering at her in the gardener's cottage.

She poured some tea, grateful for its warmth soothing her throat. Sloker had gripped her tightly in the copse and again as he had marched her through it to the cottage. His treatment of her had been nothing short of barbaric as he had roughly shoved her through the doorway. She wondered where he had found the key, but did it matter? What was done was done. She could change nothing but the future.

She sat at her vanity and stared at herself. Gone was the look of a fresh-faced woman giddy with the flush of love. In her place sat Pearl as she had been before meeting James, dark circles beneath her eyes and lacklustre hair. She sipped her tea, refusing to dwell on last night, expecting her appearance to change again once she began sleeping better at night. Although she had the sad task of burying her aunt and facing the fact she had no family left at all, she still had James. It would be all right.

He appeared in the doorway then, grey circles beneath his eyes that told of a restless night much like hers had been. She imagined him tossing and turning, alone in bed. Had he wished she was with him as she had done? When she had roused during the night to the terrible sound of silence, she had longed for him to be here, for the noise of his breathing to pierce the quiet.

She smiled at him, placed her cup and saucer on the vanity and stood, waiting for him to come to her. They remained in place for a long time, though, unspoken words and feelings crossing the space between them, and she knew without a doubt that despite her bleak past, her future would be brighter with James in it.

He broke the silence. "How are you this morning, my love?" He came into the bedroom to take her in his arms.

She pressed herself into him, smelling his calming scent and stroking her hands up and down his back. His closeness made every bad thought disappear, and he felt so *good*. "I am tired, but that is to be expected under the circumstances." With his heartbeat thudding beneath her ear, she closed her eyes. "There is so much to do, I—"

"I will help you. You are not alone in this." He threaded his fingers through her hair and massaged her scalp, his other hand at the base of her spine making lazy circles.

Pearl sighed, her burdens flying away with his words and touch. He had said the same last night before he had left, but the confirmation did not do her any harm. Uncertainty was a terrible thing when it visited in the dark of night and just as terrible when it came by day. "That man... He... I was wondering, will the murders stop now?"

"Yes, they will. There is much you are unaware of, things I kept from you to save you worry, but now he is gone I shall tell you what has happened. I just wish I had been more vigilant, but I thought him dead before he turned up here last night." He brushed his fingers over her hair, scooping it back and away from her eyes. "I felt he saw you at the club and decided you were next on his list. He said as much to me when I spoke with him."

Pearl eased away from him and looked at his face. "You *spoke* with him? When?"

James guided her to the bed, and they sat. "I sought him

172

out the other night."

His explanation followed, and Pearl gained a new understanding of how much James cared for her. For him to have found the man and warned him away touched her, then to fight with him on her property and leave him for dead in the road... He had risked being caught or seen, risked the authorities coming down on his head. All for her.

She took his hands in hers and squeezed. "I do not deserve you, James."

He smiled. "Of course you do. And you will always have me."

Frances's words came back to her then, and she asked, "Do you think he killed Luke?"

James nodded. "I would say that is a certainty. He must have questioned him as to who he waited for and lured him into giving him a ride, then killed him." He paused and stared at the ceiling. "How he got back to the club on foot so quickly eludes me. Perhaps someone gave him a lift, and he must have returned to the alley to wait for you. When I looked down onto the street it appeared he had blood on his hands, although that could have been my mind playing tricks on me, more so now because I want loose ends tied up."

She reached up to touch his cheek, threading her fingers through the hair at his temple. "He was a despicable man. I am not ashamed to admit I have no remorse that he is dead. How could I, when he killed my aunt and those poor women?" She remained quiet for a moment, then stared into his eyes and said, "Would it be terrible if I said I wanted you? Because I do. I want to be Lily. I want to be someone else. Being me hurts too much at present."

"Then you shall be a gentleman's harlot for as long as you need to be. If it means taking away your pain, I do not give a damn what is proper and what is not. You are all that is important to me."

She stood and drew up her nightgown, the material sensuous as it breezed across her skin. She straddled his

173

legs, holding the swathe of fabric below her breasts, and smiled at the sight of him gazing at her lower region. With a gentle hand to his chest, she pushed him backward and stared down at him. Lily came to the fore as she took in the breadth of his chest beneath a white shirt, the bulge below his waist, and his eyes that bored into her. A frisson of desire awakened her bud, and it throbbed, her folds growing wet. She reached forward and took his hand, guiding it to her slit.

"Do you feel how much I want you?" she asked. "I am so wet..."

He flushed, cheeks pink with high spots of colour, and his breathing quickened. He took her hand and placed it on his cock. "Do you feel how much I want *you?*"

Pearl massaged his erection, freeing it from the confining fabric. The weight of him in her hand and the softness of his skin changed her earlier frisson to raging fire. The need to obliterate all bad memories overtook her, and she got onto the bed. Knees either side of him, she positioned his tip at her entrance. Sinking down, she closed her eyes and drowned in the feeling of being filled, that delicious, slightly burning stretch. She rose and fell slowly, hands on her thighs, fingers splayed, and dug her nails into her skin. The sharp pain snapped her eyes open, and she looked down at James as he looked up at her.

"You are so beautiful," he said. "Everything I dreamed of."

He flipped them over so he lay on top of her. His weight and his face so near made Pearl want to surrender to whatever he chose to do. She flung her hands above her head and clasped them together, arching her back so her breasts pressed against him. His body warmth seeped through her skin, bringing them together as one, never to be parted.

He thrust into her with long, languid strokes, and the burn of burgeoning pleasure all but scored her folds. Snaking his hands beneath her so she was cradled in his arms, he kissed her deeply, tongue probing and firm. She returned the kiss in an almost frantic bid to transport her feelings into him. A searing tenderness gripped her, and she fought the urge to cry. This moment, this feeling…she wanted it to last forever.

Unable to keep from touching him any longer, she unclasped her hands and settled them on his lower back. Fingers sliding beneath his shirt, she trailed them up his spine, pushing him closer when her palms met his shoulder blades. He thrust harder, deeper, his wiry curls abrading her needy bud. Shots of pleasure spiralled outward to her labia, then to her core, building in intensity the more he jerked inside her. She kissed him with unabridged desire urging her towards the edge, and her stomach rolled in her excitement of falling over the chasm and soaking in bliss.

He groaned and wrenched his mouth from hers, kissing down her neck before suckling the curve where it met her shoulder. She gripped his shoulders and scooped his earlobe into her mouth, holding it lightly between her teeth and flicking it with her tongue. He groaned again, louder, hoarser, and peppered kisses down to her breast. His hot breath heated her nipple a second before he sucked it into his mouth, and she forgot everything but what he was doing.

She cried out, his attentions on her nipple creating spikes of pleasure that rippled down to join those in her cunt. His thrusts became disjointed, sharper, with more purpose, and she recognised that as him being close. Her excitement grew and she wanted to match him, gain her release at the same time.

A sweep of lust overtook her, and his pelvic movements grazing her swollen bud increased the sensations between her legs. Pearl let herself go, enjoying the sharp tugs on her nipple, the jerky jabs into her channel. Ecstasy spread throughout her folds and consumed her, a violent storm that rendered her pliant and weak. Each ebb and flow encouraged stuttered groans from her lips, soon stifled by James's mouth covering hers. He plundered her with tongue and cock, and a whimper rose up then died in her throat.

Sweat coated her skin, coated his skin, and she slid her hands easily down his back to push on the base of his spine. The heavier pressure on her pulsating nub teased out the last tendrils of pleasure, and she pulled her mouth away from his to suck in some air.

He kissed her neck, murmuring endearments into her hair, and gave a deep, hard thrust as the first jet of his seed spilled. He pummelled her quickly then, moaning her name and squeezing her to him. She held on, clutched at him, never wanting to let him go, wrapping her legs around his waist and locking her ankles.

They remained that way for some time, and before Pearl drifted off to sleep, she knew that so long as James was in her life, she could cope with anything.

Chapter Fifteen

January, 1889

The Diary of Seth Adams

I have not had much time or the inclination to write my diary since that dreadful night. I have Pearl as my own and no need to document my feelings for her as I have done in the past. Those words were there to read again and again when she was not in my life. She is here now, the mistress of my home, the woman who married me a fortnight since and made my life complete.

It is not difficult to love her or to share my home after years of living alone. It is as though she has always been here, that the previous months never existed when I slept by myself and wished she was mine. The circumstances that brought her to me are not conventional, and the events that followed our first meeting were terribly unfortunate, but I would do it all again if it meant the outcome would be the same.

At the time I took this diary from my desk drawer and opened it with pen poised above the paper to write, I questioned why I had done so. And then I thought of my beautiful love, and how, if something were to ever happen to me, she might find solace in knowing how very much I adore her. Then she, too, will have these words to read when she feels alone. Of course, I pray nothing will take me from her, but the future is never certain, and I want to ensure she has something other than memories to cherish.

So, I have decided that, rather than abandon my writing,

I shall continue year after year. My love can only grow stronger, for every day I see new things about my wife that endear her to me more. There will be many things to document — children and grandchildren, please God, and special events that happen as the years roll by. Perhaps I will not write every day as I have before, but I shall record the things that touch me deeply.

Today we are taking Annabel into the city for a treat. She needs new clothing since putting on a little weight through eating properly, and Pearl wanted to bestow some appropriate clothing upon her for when they both venture into the city or have visitors to the house. The grey dress the maid constantly wears has become thin, and to see her in a frock more becoming to her new position will make my wife happy.

I will do anything for Pearl. Anything to make her happy.

She has complained lately of feeling a little unwell, and I am hoping it means she is expecting our first child. Although this news will please me greatly, I am worried that the pregnancy and birth will take its toll on her. She is so precious to me that the fear of childbirth going wrong concerns me. I fear that my continually asking her if she is all right may wear on her, but it seems I cannot stop myself from checking. I must tell her why I am worried. Perhaps then she will understand why I have become a nuisance.

Last night she became Lily again and showed me a new side to her I wish to see again. She is insatiable when lust consumes her and changes her into someone far removed from the personality she shows others. When we are in company she is polite and demure, but in the bedroom it is another matter. I smile to myself as she offers our visitors tea and cake, knowing that the previous night she had uttered words no lady should admit to saying.

"Lick my cunt, James..."

The very thought of it makes my cock hard. As does recalling what she wanted last night.

"Chastise me, James," she said from beneath me on the

bed. "Tell me I am a naughty little wench."

I stilled inside her, my shaft stiffening further, and it took several seconds before I began thrusting again. She stared at me, her eyes half-lidded, her lips a pout, and I wondered if I could do as she asked. I had spanked women before, but not my Pearl. Not my Lily.

"Please, James. Let us try this. Just for tonight."

I rolled sentences around in my mind, trying them on for size before opening my mouth. I wanted to be sure they sounded right, to be comfortable with them. Finding words I liked, I watched her licking her lips, something she knows drives me wild, and all reservations fled.

"You have been a bad little whore, Lily," I said, grinding my hips to the rhythm of my words. "A naughty... desirable...wretched...little...whore."

Her sheath contracted with every word I spoke, and damn if I did not have to hold back from spewing my seed. God, she felt more than good. She pressed her hands down on my lower back, nails digging into the skin, and the sharp, painful sensations heightened my need. I felt I would not last much longer. She knows how to please me, what to do to ensure I lose control, as though we had been born for one another.

"Again, James. Say it again. I love it when you talk to me like that. It makes me feel so...wickedly wanton."

I upped the pace of my thrusts and ground out, "You have been...a bad little...whore. I may need...to punish you."

She smiled, the curving of her lips slow and sensual. "Hit me," she stated bluntly. "Hit me like that man hit the madam."

"He struck her?" I asked, unsure as to why I was shocked. Had I not indulged in the same with Charlotte?

"Yes, he did. And it looked so...pleasurable. The madam certainly enjoyed it. I would like to experience the same. I have thought about it many times since I witnessed it. Please, hit me. I want to know what it feels like to have you slapping me like that. Just this once. I will not ask again if I

179

do not like it or if you do not like doing it."

I could not believe my luck. I had always enjoyed spanking a woman, had paid Charlotte to accommodate my needs, but had never expected to find a life-long partner who would enjoy the same. It was unheard of, at least in my circles, for a wife to enjoy the act of sex, let alone a good, thorough spanking.

My married friends complained that once they were married and their wives had become pregnant, they were ousted from the bedroom until long after the baby was born. Until they wished for another child. I had thought, back when this snippet of information had come my way, that my club would continue to thrive if this was the way of things. Men would always want the comfort of a giving woman, and I provided the place for that service. Good God, but I did not expect my friends to be visiting my establishment. And I had never expected to find a woman like Pearl.

Taking her with me, I rolled on to my back and gripped her waist to set her moving. As she smoothed her hands up and down my chest, I gained eye contact with her and rubbed light circles on the cheeks of her arse. She sucked in air and released it in an unhurried breath. I continued rubbing, not wanting her to know when I would strike. The thought of spanking her was enticing, but I harboured a small doubt that I would hurt her and she would not like it.

"How hard do you want it, harlot? How *much* do you want it?"

She closed her eyes and groaned. "I want it to sting. And I want it so very badly. Hit me. Please, just hit me. I cannot wait much longer."

For a second I stilled my hands, astounded at how this woman never failed to amaze me. Our lovemaking had been a revelation, and the fact that Pearl loved being Lily so much gave our couplings a sharper edge. I circled her cheeks again, wanting to make her wait, to beg.

She rode me, the wavy sheet of her red hair almost

covering her face. Tossing her head back, she exposed her slender neck, her prominent collarbones, and I was undone. Quickly, I sat up and ran my tongue over the bones, down into the hollow between them, tasting her unique taste, the tang of her perfume mixed with the sweat our lovemaking had so far produced. I lifted one hand from her arse and brought it back down with a hard strike, the contact of skin on skin smarting my palms.

She cried out and looked at me, eyes wide with shock even though she had expected the slap. I knew she had not realised it would be quite so sharp.

"Do you want more, or is that enough?" I asked, my breathing ragged and my heart beating wildly.

She bit her lower lip and circled her hips before replying. "More. A little harder."

I did as she asked, smacking her soundly twice in a row. She moaned and leant down to kiss me, her tongue seeking to touch every inner surface of my mouth. I returned her fervour, bollocks tender with my need for release. I would have to give in soon. It was becoming impossible not to. Her breasts pressed against me, the hardness of her nipples a stark contrast to the softness of her fleshy swells.

She broke the kiss. "Do that again," she breathed. "With both hands. And take me from behind."

That nearly unravelled me.

She climbed off me and stood beside the bed, planting her palms on the mattress. "The madam did this. She stood this way, and the man, he... He rammed inside her, slapped her hard on the thighs. He...it was... Oh, just fuck me from behind and slap me!"

I shot out of bed. I had to touch her, feel her skin on mine. I stood behind her, grabbed her waist and plunged my cock deep. The position changed the feel of her sheath. It was tighter this way, and I could push in farther. God, she was a surprising delight, this wife of mine, and I wanted to fuck her ragged until she begged for me to take her over the edge. With quick thrusts making her breasts bounce, I closed my eyes and listened to the slap of our bodies. God, how I loved that sound.

"Come on, James! Slap me!"

Her impatience stiffened my cock some more, and I fought the desire to shoot inside her. Instead, I focused on rubbing her outer thighs, priming them for the strikes to come. She pushed back against me, sending me deeper still, and my balls throbbed painfully as I denied myself release.

I worked faster, pumping her channel, and lifted my hands high, bringing them down at the same time, one on each thigh. Pearl shrieked and panted, low groans following soon after. That she had enjoyed it pushed me over the edge, and the telltale throb of the vein in my cock began.

I smacked her again, saying, "You naughty, naughty wench."

She keened, a sound I found myself loving. I slapped her harder so I could hear it again. She obliged, this time the noise long and full, as though she had dredged it from the depths of her belly. Her skin heated my palms, made them itch and tingle, and I risked one more set of slaps to each thigh. She jerked her head up, panting, and loud, juddering groans pierced the air.

My excitement grew to a dangerous level. I pulled out of her, spun her around, and gently pushed her back onto the bed. I climbed on top of her, spearing her cunt, but she had other ideas as to our position. She gripped the tops of my arms and whipped me onto my back, keeping me inside her the whole time.

With her seated on me that way, I was able to stare at her lush, full breasts. I reached out to fondle them, to tweak her hard nipples until she cried out her pleasure. She closed her eyes and dragged her nails down my chest, then placed one on my shoulder for balance while her other sought out her folds. I had wanted to watch her touch herself but had not asked in case it made her uncomfortable. She was far from that, it seemed, and circled over her bud. Her fingertips brushed me as she rose and fell, and I drank in the sight before me.

Who would have thought this woman, this quiet, proper woman would have been such a hellcat in bed? I most certainly would not have believed it unless I had seen it with my own eyes. She continued to caress herself, tongue slipping out to trace the seam of her lips, and the memory of what that tongue felt like as she took my cock into her mouth and sucked upward almost had me coming.

"James, this feels so good. It is so…ah, I could fuck you all day."

My God, she never failed to shock me with her choice of words. Even though she had said them before, she had used them more often of late. Her feeling comfortable enough with me to utter them like she did was testament to the trust we shared, and a surge of love for her swept through me, so vast it prevented me from breathing for a moment.

"Yes, that is good," she whispered, eyes closed. She pleasured herself faster, rubbing up and down with the tips of two fingers then changing direction, circling her bud with pressured strokes. "You inside me, and me touching myself. God, James, slap me again. Just one more time."

I groaned then raised my hands, bringing them down hard and fast on her arse cheeks. She screamed out, and my seed shot up my shaft and out, filling her with wet heat. She groaned out her pleasure as she squeezed my cock and her torso bucked. Her breasts swayed, and I reached up to hold them in my palms while she emptied me. Thumbs brushing her nipples, I closed my eyes and savoured the heady sensations. My head lightened, and my chest constricted through lack of air as I held my breath.

The pleasure was more heightened than our previous couplings, the newness of Pearl wanting to be slapped bringing a stronger desire. She was everything I had dreamed of and more, and I could only imagine how much more she would bring to the bedroom in the future. From what I had seen so far, she was not afraid to experiment.

Pearl slowed to a stop and leant down to kiss me again. My chest heaved as I breathed through my nose to steady my fast-beating heart. With her fingers in my hair, we took the time to come down from the sexual high we had experienced.

A little later, with Pearl on her tummy, I massaged a cooling lotion into her buttocks and arse. The pink skin looked sore, but she assured me it had been worth it.

"Perhaps next time you would chastise me?"

She lifted her head to try and look at me over her shoulder, hair a mess over most of her face. "Me chastise you?"

"Why not? If I do not like it, we need not do it again."

She let her head fall back down on to her folded arms, and I continued to attend to her bottom, wondering how those hard slaps had felt, how they would feel when she gave them to me.

"You would have to wait until Lily wants to play," she murmured.

"I will wait," I said. "I waited long enough for you before, and I will wait again."

* * * *

February 5th, 1889

Pearl stared out the drawing room window at the frost on the grass and smiled. When the weather changed from cold snaps to hotter days, she would be close to giving birth. She had discovered her pregnancy a week ago and looked forward to the coming months as her body shape changed and the child she had created with James wriggled inside her. He had fretted when she had told him the news, as she had known he would, but after he had spoken with a physician on the subject, his mind had been put somewhat at rest.

He appeared at the end of the drive, guiding their new carriage towards the house, the horse pulling it a pretty chestnut with a white mane and tail. Smiling wider, she left

184

the window and went to the front door to watch him draw up to the house and show off the new purchase.

James jumped down from his seat, and she absorbed the sight of him as though she had not seen him in an age. She always felt like this when they spent any amount of time apart. Whenever he left, she felt as though he took a huge chunk of her with him. She was so lucky to have found a man who suited her so perfectly. To have found a man at all when she had resigned herself to being left on the shelf.

He patted the horse, beckoning her over with a flick of his hand, a broad smile forming. "What do you think?"

She stepped on to the gravel and approached him, giving him a long, deep kiss, servants watching through windows be damned. They ought to be used to their public displays of affection by now, and if any of them did not like it they could always leave. That sounded harsh, but Pearl was not going to hide how she felt about her husband in her own home. Oh, they did not go overboard, but they did not act like Elizabeth and Gerald, who remained apart when visiting, never holding hands or smiling in that secret way Pearl and James did.

She pulled away and smiled, looking him in the eye, so pleased he was home. "I missed you." She reached up to stroke his cheek, the stubble there rasping against her palm.

"But I have been gone only a few hours," he said with a chuckle.

"A few hours too long." With reluctance, she turned to the horse and offered her palm for the beast to sniff. "The carriage is lovely, and the horse is beautiful. Male or female?"

"Male. Can you not see?" He grinned. "You must name him." He kissed her cheek then tucked a stray tress of hair behind her ear, an act she found endearing.

She eyed the horse. "Later. Now I just want you indoors. I have missed you more than usual today."

"The brewery can run itself tomorrow with Kenneth in charge. How does that sound?"

"Wonderful. Perhaps we could give the staff here the day off," she whispered. "Maybe I will wake up as Lily and we can be free to indulge throughout the house. Imagine that. You can take me over the dining room table." She walked closer to him, rested her cheek against his, and lowered her voice. "You can fuck me from behind, if you like. Or sit me on the counter in the kitchen and fuck me there. Or take me in the bathroom…"

"Oh, God, Pearl. You have no idea what you do to me, woman."

"If it is anything like what you do to me, I have a fair idea." She smiled, knowing what she would say next. "You could even lick my cunt as I sit on the stairs."

His breathing quickened, and she moved closer. He groaned, licking her earlobe, and the sound of his pleasure brought gooseflesh to her skin. Before they did something they would regret, she stepped back so they were feet apart. He adjusted his coat to hide his excitement and stared at her, lust in his eyes.

His flushed cheeks and wide smile warmed her folds, the possibility of her being Lily tonight enticing.

"I shall put the carriage away and stable the horse, then inform the staff that tomorrow is their lucky day."

"It will be yours too," she said.

"From what you have said, I am sure it will be. But every day is my lucky day."

Pearl's eyes misted, and she struggled to see him clearly. "I adore you, James. Please say you will never leave me."

"Never," he said, bringing her to his chest and kissing the top of her head. "I will never leave you. We have so much to look forward to. So many years."

"And will we enjoy every one?"

"Of course. There is no doubt in my mind."

With her cheek against his chest, Pearl stared out over the grounds, so much bigger than those of her childhood home. She allowed herself a few moments to dwell on the past then shut the terrible memories away, enjoying a life where the man holding her close loved her unconditionally. Her dream had finally come true.

She lifted her head and looked up at him. "Lily is on her way."

"Oh, Lord. Please, hold her off until I have settled the horse."

She gave him a wicked grin and walked backward to the front steps. "Do not leave her waiting too long. You know how hungry she gets. I will be in the bedroom."

"And I will not be far behind, my love."

The Submissive's Secret

Excerpt

Chapter One

Diary, October 7th

"Will you come clubbing with us tonight, Lori?" Fiona had asked.

I'd shaken my head, as usual.

Friday nights were reserved for something else entirely.

"Why not?" she'd asked. "You never come out with us now. Got yourself a secret man, have you?"

How did I answer something I didn't want to answer? How did I tell her that on Friday nights I did something they just wouldn't understand? How the hell did I remain polite when, because I was being pushed on a regular basis by my work colleagues, I wanted to tell her to leave it, please, just leave it?

I'd shrugged. "Just a bit busy, that's all."

"Doing what?"

"Things."

"What things?"

I'd smiled, thinking of what I'd be doing. "Just things."

I'd got up, walked away from the packed table, and Fiona had said to the others, "What's she hiding? What's her secret?"

I'd left the pub. My 'secret' was a secret for a reason. I hid what I hid for a reason. What I did on Friday nights was something just for me. My thing.

And I wasn't going to share it with anyone except my Swedish Dom.

* * * *

I sensed him behind me, my Dom, and resisted turning around to look at him. This week had dragged, my need to be with him seeming to make the days crawl by slower. I remained staring at the optics behind the bar, paying the label on a bottle of vodka particular attention, my senses buzzing.

Orchestral music filtered through speakers set high in every corner, a soft, haunting melody I'd always associate with him. Jaska, the man who had so far met my every need, whom I'd learnt to trust like no other.

"What are you doing in a place like this, pet?"

His voice had flowed effortlessly with the music, as though he'd sung the words. My stomach muscles tightened—excitement, so much excitement inside me—and I swallowed in an attempt to calm the rapid-fire flash of butterflies' wings in my windpipe.

They fluttered on. They always did.

"I'm here to meet my Master," I said.

I sat rigid, dying to swivel on the barstool and face him. To take in his beautiful face, the way his cheekbones tapered towards his jaw—a jaw that some people would say was glass, so finely sculpted that it appeared fragile. It was always coated with stubble—God, I loved that—the darkness of it a shade blacker than his short hair.

"I see." He placed a hand on my shoulder.

I shivered with delight, unable to hide it, and imagined him smiling.

"And your Master," he said, "has been waiting for you. Over there, in the corner. He saw you come in, had the urge to get up and meet you straight away, to greet you like a lover, but that wouldn't do, would it? We've never worked like that."

"No," I said.

"But at some point..." He squeezed my shoulder, as though reassuring himself I was still there. "At some point things *will* have to change, you know that. It's always been there between us, that knowledge. Sometimes I think I'll go mad thinking about it."

I'd been dreading this moment ever since I'd met him eight months ago. That he'd have to set me free, let me experience the BDSM world with others, express myself. He'd said once—about five months ago if I remember correctly—that he was enjoying showing me the ropes more than any other sub he'd trained. I'd laughed at that—he'd shown me more than just ropes—and thought to myself that it would be ages before I'd have to face what was ahead. Time, though, was a cruel bitch, and she'd swept by too fast, turning weeks into months, drawing the inevitable closer. I'd told myself to be strong, that I could handle whatever came my way since Jaska had come into in my life. But I'd been fooling myself.

Not having him in my life? No, I didn't want to contemplate that.

I held my breath then let it out slowly. "Which way will they change?" I hadn't even needed to ask that question. I knew the answer, but a part of me wanted to see if anything was different now that we'd spent so many Friday nights together.

"That's entirely up to you, pet. What do you see as your options?"

Entirely up to me? Well, *that* was different. I hadn't been aware of any options other than the one he'd stated from the start. "I only have one, as far as I'm concerned, but it might not be what you want to hear. It isn't the one you gave me."

"I asked you a question and you didn't answer it. If I didn't want to hear, I wouldn't have asked. Games, you know I dislike them, Lori. We made promises. Say what we have to say, no playing about. It works better for both of us that way. We know where we stand. I'm a little saddened you've forgotten that rule."

I stiffened. His disappointment in me, albeit very mild, had been evident.

"I hadn't forgotten," I said. "But it isn't as cut and dried as it was. When emotions get involved, they're not so easily switched off, are they?"

"They could be, if you're a particularly strong person."

"And you are, Sir?"

"I thought I was, yes."

I frowned. Was he trying to tell me something? Was he breaking his own rule and 'playing about'?

"Now who isn't saying what he has to say?" I said boldly.

"We need to talk, I see. So, let's talk. Here. Now. Answer my first question."

I sighed, let my shoulders slump. This wasn't going to be easy to confess. The outcome wouldn't be what I wanted. I'd be sent out into the lifestyle, feeling as though I'd been scattered to the four winds. Lost. Adrift. And so alone. The lifestyle for me, without him in it, wouldn't be the same.

"My only option has always been that you would teach me, help me to understand how a Dom works, how I work as a sub, and then you'd let me go. I wasn't aware there were any other options. But I do have another, and it's the only one I can imagine. To have only you as my Master. I don't want anyone else."

There. I've said it.

I held my breath again, the vodka label gauzy now, the music swelling to a crescendo. He squeezed my shoulder again, and I waited for his sigh of impatience. It would tell me everything I needed to know.

It didn't come.

"Do you feel the teaching process is over, then?" he asked.

"Yes. I know what I want now, you've shown me that. Taught me that."

"You don't feel you've become attached to me just because of what we've shared? That happens, you know. Subs think they love their teachers, when in fact it's just an emotional tether that holds them together. Easily broken when they find someone else."

"Fuck, no!" I said, closing my eyes, erasing the sight of that damn label, and hating myself for blurting out like that.

What was it I'd said? *When emotions get involved...* Oh, God, how had it come to this so soon? It wasn't meant to happen for another four months. A year, he'd said. One year to teach me, then he'd set me free.

"You believe you care about me?" he asked.

"I love you. Sir." I hadn't meant to say that, not yet, but it had seemed natural. Right. This evening might well end sooner than it usually did. How quickly life changed direction. I'd got ready to meet him earlier, full of joy that tonight was actually here, and now look.

He did sigh then and took his hand from my shoulder. "Turn to me, pet."

I bit my bottom lip and swivelled around, eyes still closed, head bowed. There was no question of my ignoring his request—I always obeyed him. What would it be like to no longer hear his commands? How the hell would I manage when kneeling alone at home, naked, knowing it was for no reason at all except an action played out from habit? He wouldn't call me at the appointed time to ask if I'd tuned in to my inner self and thought of him—only him—and what he was going to teach me next.

He slid his finger beneath my chin, raised my face, and I could only imagine his expression. Frowning—yes, I thought he'd be frowning, wondering how he was going to break it to me that he didn't love me, that he'd taught so many women and the only way forward was to cut ties. He didn't do attachment. He didn't do love. How could I have been so stupid as to think I'd be the woman to change that? Had I believed I'd be different? The One?

"Look at me, Lori."

I opened my eyes and stared into his, which always took my breath away. They bordered on black, tiny grey flecks darting in from the outer rim only to fade near the centre, the pupils lost in the surrounding darkness. I held back the sudden onset of tears. They could come later, when I was by myself. And as for my lip threatening to tremble... I could only be glad I'd secured it between my teeth.

"We have the same dilemma, pet." He smiled, barely, an almost upwards tilt at the corners of his mouth. "I don't want to let you go any more than you want me to."

I shook my head a little in disbelief. I hadn't heard him right. I'd heard what I'd wanted to, and in reality he'd probably said he *had* to let me go.

That our contract was binding.

"Are you all right?" he asked, tilting his head, eyes narrowed in a way I'd come to know as concern.

I cleared my throat. "Please say that again, Sir."

"I don't want to let you go. Didn't you hear my slip earlier? What I'd said?"

I thought back to the start of our conversation.

"He saw you come in, had the urge to get up and meet you straight away, to greet you like a lover..."

"I...it didn't register," I said. "I thought it was just part of the game. We always meet like this, talk like that. I just didn't..."

He smiled wider, still a soft curve, but the sight of it mellowed the butterflies' flight from frantic to gentle. I felt less coiled, but it would take a while before I calmed completely. Our conversation had taken a turn I'd only dreamt about and I wasn't sure how to deal with it. I knew what I *wanted* to do—fling myself off the stool and into his arms – but doing so in here, with other people as witnesses, wasn't something I thought I could do. It had to be private, didn't it, a moment like that.

"I've had the advantage," he said, "of having taught other subs, of knowing that emotions born of trust may well have nothing to do with love. But with you… Ah, my beautiful sub, it's been so very different."

His voice, had it really cracked? Had his accent become thicker?

"I don't know what to say," I whispered, pulse fluctuating madly in my neck. "I can't quite believe – "

"Believe it," he said. "If you're willing, I want to collar you. I have the burning need to make you mine, to *show* that you're mine. However…"

He ran his thumb across my chin, a back-and-forth motion that set those wings to flapping faster inside me. Just a slight touch, a simple touch, and he had me wet, wanting to do anything – *anything* – he asked me to. No, I couldn't be without him. Not now. We'd done so much, gone so far.

He doesn't want to let me go.

I was flooded with that knowledge then and battled to remain in control. "However…?"

"I needed to be sure you knew what you wanted. If you'd have told me you looked forward to being free in the lifestyle after our year had ended, so be it. I wouldn't want to stand in your way. But collaring. It's a big thing, as I've told you. It's very real, very binding."

"I understand, Sir. I want what you want."

He nodded then dipped his head. The kiss he brushed onto my lips was so light I could be forgiven for thinking it hadn't happened. But they burned, those lips of mine, the fire streaking from them straight down to my cunt. We had a connection, me and Jaska, one I couldn't imagine sharing with any other man.

"You must understand," he said, "that a little kiss like that, with you, could send a man off kilter."

I smiled, my eyes watery. I blinked to clear my vision,

not wanting it distorted so I couldn't see his face clearly. I wanted to take in every micro-expression that flitted across it, to savour this moment, to allow myself to fully understand that his offer of one year had perhaps extended to a lifetime.

"It's the same for me, with you," I said. "I can't imagine kissing anyone else."

He traced his thumb over my lips, and I went with instinct and dashed my tongue out to lick it.

"And that," he said, "is exactly why I love you. Why things are different with you. The other subs waited to be told to do things like that. Whereas you… My girl, you are such a perfect match for me."

"The contract," I said. "It doesn't apply anymore."

"No, it does not. I have another. Here, in my suit pocket. Just in case, you understand."

I nodded. He'd been unsure, then, hadn't let himself believe I could love him any more than I'd thought he could love me.

"When will I sign it, Sir?"

"In a moment. When we go to our room. I just need to look at you first. For a moment, so I can…"

"Can what?" I blinked again—damn those prickling tears—and swallowed.

"So I can take it in, that you're still here, that you want what I want."

He'd revealed something to me of which he was perhaps unaware. Although a Dom, he still faltered, was still unsure at times. I had thought, because he'd always been so strong, so in control, that he had every eventuality covered. I realised that I had so much more to learn. I'd forgotten that underneath the somewhat hard outer shell he'd presented to me, he was a person underneath.

A man. With feelings.

Feelings towards me.

If I wasn't so mesmerised by his eyes, by the swipe-swipe-swipe of his thumb, by his unsteady breathing, by that beautiful tweak of his lips, I would have lifted one hand to pinch myself.

Chapter Two

Diary, October 8th

Last night wrung me out emotionally, and I was glad we hadn't entered play. It wouldn't have been the same. Jaska had said we should take some time to go through the new contract, for me to fully understand what he required of me and what I should expect from him. I'd been ready to sign it whatever it had contained, but as usual, he'd been right. Emotions were dangerous things, he'd said. They clouded judgement and made you do things you wouldn't ordinarily do.

He'd explained about collaring before – had explained every aspect of the lifestyle in the eight months he'd been teaching me – but had gone through it again so things were clear. Then he'd confessed he'd already bought a collar. Just in case, he'd said, and had smiled sheepishly, reminding me once again that he had emotions, feelings that would present themselves more and more in the coming months and years.

It was a relief to know that in four months I didn't have to say goodbye unless I chose to. That our time together was never-ending as long as that was what we both wanted. In our room he'd confessed – his voice a whisper that had held a tremor, his hand suffering much the same as he'd placed his palm to my cheek – that he'd never been in love before. That this was all so new to him that he'd been having a difficult time getting to grips with it.

I'd known hearts could melt, mine had done so with him before, but in that moment? My God, its solidity had disappeared and had become a liquid mass that churned and jostled inside me, a great wave that threatened to take out the butterflies.

I'd left the club, not in a taxi arranged by him, as was our usual ritual, but in his car. He drove a sleek Mercedes, black exterior, tan leather inside, and it had spoken volumes of who he was, that he had a pretty penny or two. I hadn't seen the car before last night, knew nothing personal about him except that he worked in an office in the city. I knew him for him, plain and simple, and perhaps him falling for me had been because of that.

I most certainly wasn't after him for his money.

He'd dropped me home, walked me to my doorstep like a gentleman, and kissed me as we stood on the step, me on tiptoes so my mouth could reach his.

I don't have to wait until next Friday to see him now. It'll take some time for me to get used to that. You know, seeing him most nights instead.

I've thought it before, but God, how swiftly life can change.

* * * *

The air was a little chilly. I'd forgotten to turn the heating up a bit before I'd undressed and knelt in the middle of my living room. Still, it was too late now. The time to kneel had come, and I wasn't going to get up for anyone or anything.

Unless it was for Jaska.

With my hands clasped behind me at the small of my back, me resting on my haunches, head bowed, I did as I'd been instructed and thought about last night and what it meant for the future. Jaska had said that I'd need this time of meditation, to make sure I knew what entering that new contract with him entailed. It was simple, the rules set out clearly, and if at any time I was uncomfortable, I only had to say. He'd always encouraged me to speak up, to tell him what I wanted and needed, otherwise how would he know?

Having been denied orgasm last night, and me denying myself all week in anticipation of seeing him, my need for release—for him to touch me, lick me, whip me, hurt me— was now bordering on painful. My clit throbbed, and as I clenched my internal muscles to try to stop desire building, my cunt seeped wetness.

If only he were here now.

Instead of thinking about the contract, I let myself float to other things, visuals that would torment me, make me want to come. Our past filtered into my mind, of how, when I'd first walked into the club—an obvious newbie playing at being an experienced sub—he'd been the only one to approach me. The only Dom without a sub that night.

Had fate played a hand?

We'd spent the evening in the bar, him asking me what I expected from my visits, from a Dom, should one decide to take me on. I'd been instantly attracted to him, so much so it had caught me off guard. Something had hummed between us, the air going fuzzy with need and want, desire and so many other things my head had spun. He'd ended the evening by offering me a chance to be taught by him, sending me away to think about it, and that if I was still willing a week later to meet him there, at the same spot, then we would begin.

Nerves had gripped me all week, but I'd returned. Oh, yes, I'd returned.

My phone rang, jolting me out of my trip down memory lane. It could only be Jaska. I glanced at the screen, the phone in front of me on the hardwood floor. His name was displayed in white font against my screensaver background, a coil of silver chains. I'd taken the picture in our club room, the chains having been discarded on the floor after Jaska had taken them off my wrists and ankles. They'd made me think that I might like to see them again, but I wasn't sure whether our session had been the only one where we'd use them.

As I'd taught myself, I leant forward to press the answer button with the tip of my nose. Once in position with my hands behind my back, I never wanted to unclasp them until the hour session was up. Jaska had asked why I did that, and I'd told him it was a self-imposed rule that I wanted to maintain, just to see if I could.

With the phone always set to loudspeaker before I began these sessions, I said, "Hello, Sir."

"Good morning, pet."

My stomach rolled, and I closed my eyes to better indulge in the delicious sensations coursing through me — sensations only his voice could produce. My skin prickled with goosebumps, and my clit expanded, flickering with a furious beat that sent me lightheaded.

"You're in position," he said — not a question, never a question. He knew I was, that I wouldn't lie.

"Yes, Sir."

"And you've been giving our new relationship some thought."

"I started to, Sir, but my mind drifted."

"To?"

"When we'd first met."

"Ah. So we've been thinking along the same lines today. I trust they were happy memories?"

I sensed the hope in his voice and once again realised that he was in uncharted waters, what with him not having been in love before. I felt for him. For someone usually so in control, it must be difficult to have his emotions wrenched like this, to want to remain a Dom, all he'd ever known, but at the same time experience all the joys love had to give, freely and without restraint. Without the rules.

More books from
Natalie Dae

Pain of the pleasurable variety was all I needed – and Master Zum provided it.

I was addicted to Master Red as much as he seemed to be addicted to me...

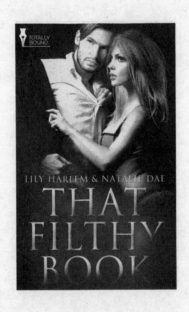

Many years ago that filthy book imprinted itself in my erotic subconscious.

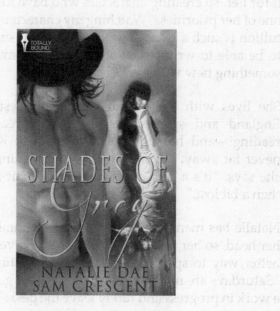

She's everything Travis Williams has ever wanted.

About the Author

Natalie Dae is a multi-published author in three pen names writing in several genres. Natalie writes mainly BDSM erotica. She loves a Dom/sub relationship and is fascinated by how it all works. The trust issue is the best thing about it for her, so creating characters who have to adopt trust is one of her priorities. "Watching my characters bloom under tuition is such a treat," she says. "I find it such a privilege to be able to write about something that makes me learn something new with every book."

She lives with her husband and youngest daughter in England and spends her spare time reading—always reading!—and her phone, complete with Kindle app, is never far away. "I can't imagine not reading or writing," she says. "It's a part of who I am. Without it I'd be more than a bit lost."

Natalie has many more BDSM tales swimming around in her head, so her workload for the future is very full. "What better way to spend a weekend than writing?" she says. "Saturdays are my main writing days, so I get up, open up a work in progress and rarely leave the desk. Unless I really have to!"

She writes at weekends and is a cover artist/head of art in her day job. In another life she was an editor. Her other pen names are Geraldine O'Hara and Sarah Masters. Natalie also co-authors as Sarah Masters with Jaime Samms, and she co-authors with Lily Harlem under the name Harlem Dae.

Natalie Dae loves to hear from readers. You can find contact information, website details and an author profile page at https://www.totallybound.com/

Bristol, May 14, 15: Gloucestershire 131 & 158, Yorkshire 234 (G.Pepall 5-63, C.L.Townsend 5-67) & 57-1. *Won by nine wickets*

Bradford, May 18, 19, 20: Yorkshire 543 (E.Wainwright 145, R.Peel 111) & 22-0, Sussex 265 & 296 (K.S.Ranjitsinhji 138). *Won by ten wickets*

Lord's, May 21, 22, 23: Middlesex 384 (H.B.Hayman 152, A.E.Stoddart 100) & 142 (R.Peel 6-28), Yorkshire 381 (J.T.Brown 203, J.T.Hearne 7-104) & 147-0. *Won by ten wickets*

Headingley, May 28, 29, 30: Kent 205 (F.Marchant 128) & 275, Yorkshire 459 (Lord Hawke 110*, A.Hearne 5-125) & 23-1. *Won by nine wickets*

Trent Bridge, June 1, 2, 3: Yorkshire 450 (J.T.Brown 107), Nottinghamshire 279 & 328. *Match drawn*

Bradford, June 8, 9, 10: Yorkshire 135 (G.A.Lohmann 7-61) & 134-7dec, Surrey 147 & 75-6. *Match drawn*

Bradford, June 11, 12: Essex 109 (E.Wainwright 6-43) & 55 (E.Wainwright 8-34), Yorkshire 80 (F.G.Bull 8-44) & 85-3. *Won by seven wickets*

Leicester, June 18, 19, 20: Yorkshire 660 (J.T.Brown 131, G.H.Hirst 107), Leicestershire 165 (G.H.Hirst 5-67) & 193. *Won by an innings and 302 runs*

Derby, June 25, 26, 27: Yorkshire 416 & 43-1, Derbyshire 281 (W.Storer 100) & 450-8dec (H.Bagshaw 115, W.Storer 100*). *Match drawn*

Sheffield, July 2, 3, 4: Yorkshire 298 (D.Denton 113, J.J.Hulme 5-80) & 86-1, Derbyshire 151 (S.Haigh 6-45) & 232 (W.Storer 122, S.Haigh 6-70). *Won by nine wickets*

Headingley, July 6, 7: Warwickshire 167 & 148 (S.Haigh 7-49), Yorkshire 329. *Won by an innings and 14 runs*

Huddersfield, July 9, 10, 11: Nottinghamshire 226 & 58-6, Yorkshire 90 (S.Brown 6-56) & 193. *Lost by four wickets*

Leyton, July 13, 14, 15: Yorkshire 203 (F.G.Bull 7-73) & 133 (C.G.Kortright 5-56), Essex 205 (S.Haigh 5-77) & 134-6. *Lost by four wickets*

Southampton, July 16, 17, 18: Hampshire 515 (E.G.Wynyard 268), Yorkshire 307 & 235-8 (T.Soar 7-97). *Match drawn*

Headingley, July 21, 22, 23: Yorkshire 190 (A.W.Mold 5-94) & 209 (A.W.Mold 6-67), Lancashire 169 (S.Haigh 5-55) & 107 (R.Peel 5-29). *Won by 123 runs*

Dewsbury, July 23, 24: Yorkshire 251, Somerset 78 (S.Haigh 6-38) & 167 (R.Peel 6-45). *Won by an innings and 6 runs*